TI AMO
SORRENTO
(I Love Sorrento)

MAZ CALADINE

This book is a work of fiction. The names, characters and incidents portrayed in it are the work of the author's imagination. Any resemblance to actual persons living or dead, events or localities is entirely coincidental

Dedicated to everyone who loves Sorrento and the Amalfi Coast

CONTENTS

Prologue

As the day turned into night, the outline of mount Vesuvius became more dominant. The brilliant pink and peach streaks of the sunset had turned to grey and lilac, and the beautiful sunny day was disappearing. Lights appeared in the distance, and Naples resembled a diamond necklace set against a velvet background. Sorrento was full of the sounds of laughter. The chatter of tourists mixed with the strains of Neapolitan music gave the town an exciting buzz. People were heading out for a walk down its colourful streets, stopping at bars and restaurants to enjoy a meal or drinks whilst watching the world go by.

A few kilometres away, high on the hillside, stood a lonely silhouette. A man shrouded in mystery and anxiety dripping from every pore in his body edged towards the cliff top. He stared down at the sea as it lapped against the rugged rocks. Moving forward as though preparing to jump, something stopped him. Hesitating for a moment, he fell to his knees and sobbed.

Why, in such a beautiful setting, would someone feel so distraught and sad?

What had he seen that had prevented him from jumping to his death?

THE PASSENGERS

MARTHA ADDINGTON   **Aged 84**

EVA JOHNSON   **Aged 22**

JOHN EVANS   **Aged 42**

SAM MARRIOTT   **Aged 33**

MARY SMITH   **Aged 40**

MARTHA

A sleek limousine arrived punctually outside the tall three-storey townhouse in an exclusive street in London. The sky, which had been threatening rain, decided now was the time to start its downpour. Reaching for a large umbrella, the driver headed for the elegant front door.

"Come in. I am almost ready," the elderly lady said as she opened the door to reveal an interior featured in many articles from high society magazines. "I'm just giving final instructions to my removal men. I won't be a moment."

He stood inside the doorway and gazed around. This lady had style, he thought to himself, as he observed the brightly coloured hallway, which was beautifully decorated in the warm hues of the Mediterranean. Hand-painted murals of grapevines and orange and lemon trees adorned the soft green walls, complementing the pale grey marble floor, which led to a winding staircase of the same colour and texture. Martha reappeared. She was wearing a stylish navy blue suit with a flowing orange silk scarf around her neck. Her silver-white hair, cut in a fashionable style of loose curls, complimented her attractive features. At eighty-four, she was still a beautiful woman. Only the mahogany walking stick with its silver handle hinted at her fragility. Her face lit up with a warming smile. The driver couldn't stop himself from smiling back at her.

"This is my luggage," she said as she pointed to a couple of light cream leather suitcases that contained her most important memories. Beautiful designer vintage clothes she used to wear to grand occasions with her late husband, together with her jewellery, letters, and photographs. Everything else was being forwarded to her new home.

"Let me help you to the car, madam. I'm afraid it's raining heavily."

She laughed, a lovely tinkling sound, and said.

"I love rain. I will miss it and this place, so many memories." She turned and glanced around, knowing that she would never be back to the house, which had been her home for over sixty years, and a tear pricked her eyes. '*Pull yourself together, Martha, face the future,*' she whispered to herself.

Sensing this was a special moment for her, the driver stretched out his arm to offer support, and without a backward glance, Martha was quickly on her way to the airport and her new life in Italy.

EVA

Eva glanced at the departure board. Her flight to Naples wasn't listed. Heading for the information desk, she was told check-in details would be on the board shortly. She sat down to wait. Nerves were beginning to affect her. Breathing deeply, she let her mind drift back to the moment a few weeks ago when she had made a startling discovery, which had shaken her to the core and led her to this journey. In her mother's bedroom, she found a letter hidden in an old photo frame. It was addressed to a Signor Francesco Pascali, No 2 Fisherman's Cottage, Marina Grande, Sorrento, Italy. Inside was a faded coloured photograph. She'd looked at the face of the young man, noting his striking features. '*What a handsome guy,*' she thought. '*I wonder who he is?*' It soon became apparent, as she read the letter, that he was her biological father.

Her mother's slow decline, following the death of her husband, changed Eva's life. She had become her mum's carer, administering her medications and making sure she ate properly. During this time, Eva discovered a love of cooking and spent her free time experimenting. And then the terrible day when she arrived home from school to find her mother dead on the floor from an overdose. That was five years ago.

After the funeral, the solicitor informed her that the family home had been left to her, together with a small inheritance of money. The next day, she began stripping the house of clutter.

Each room she painted white, except for the kitchen. This became bright yellow and orange, with splashes of vivid blue and lime green paint. On one wall hung a garden trellis and a plastic grapevine, with fairy lights draped in between, adding atmosphere. It inspired her to cook and experiment with food.

On an impulse, Eva ditched her A-level studies and signed up for catering college. Four years later she graduated with honours in professional cookery. Sadly, there was no one to share her achievement.

She was alone… and then she found the letter and her life changed.

In the crowded concourse, she watched as couples held hands and children shouted excitedly to each other.

Everyone seemed happy except herself. The board illuminated the flight to Naples and, picking up her bag, she quickly headed for the check-in desk and a journey that she hoped would resolve the mystery of who her biological father was and whether she could contact him.

JOHN

John closed his front door and double-checked it was locked. He glanced up and down the street to make sure no one was watching him. Carefully placing his hand-stitched leather suitcase into the boot of the taxi, he instructed the driver to take him to Heathrow Airport.

He wasn't a man to show much emotion, but today he felt nervous. This trip was so important. It had to be successful. If he failed to get a substantial order, God knows what his next move would be.

"Are you heading somewhere nice?" the taxi driver inquired of his passenger.

"Naples," John replied sharply, not wanting to engage in conversation.

"Naples, eh! When I was in the Navy, I was based there. It's a rough place. Not sure I'd want to go there for a holiday."

"I'm not going on holiday. I have a business meeting."

"Ah well, that's different," the taxi driver replied as he increased his speed to merge onto the busy dual carriageway.

John's thoughts went to the hastily arranged meeting. Signor Bartolino had been a hard man to get hold of. He just hoped this influential buyer would love his leather designs. If he got an order from this guy, then all his problems would be over. Maybe he could employ some staff, which would take the pressure off. After he left the army, he had worked non-stop to get his business going. He was determined to succeed. Gazing out of the window he allowed his dreams of being successful to flow over him.

"Here we are, mate." The driver said as he pulled into the departure area. "We were lucky the traffic wasn't too busy. Good luck with your appointment."

John thanked him. With his suitcase and portfolio firmly in his grip, he headed for the check-in desk. It was make or break time.

SAMANTHA

Samantha arrived at the airport on time. Her thoughts filled with anxiety about the trip ahead. At the check-in desk, she waited in the queue. Her heart was thumping as she placed her suitcase on the scales.

"Your bag is 3 kilos overweight madam, you need to take some items out." The airport official said. She resorted to her false smile, but was thinking, '*why don't people understand the rules.*' The times she had to repeat these words.

Samantha dragged her bag away from the desk. A feeling of panic crept in. Her eyes were filling with tears. A year ago, Robbie, her husband, had died of cancer and, in his last moments and to ease his anxiety, she agreed to scatter his ashes in Italy. They had married in the Cloisters in Sorrento, and she knew how much it had meant to him.

The Italian Consulate had refused permission for Robbie's ashes to be scattered in Italy. She was devastated. However, they would allow her to transport them in a sealed casket for internment at the local cemetery. As far as Sam was concerned, this was not an option.

She sat on the floor. Her long, flowing olive green skirt giving some added cover as she transferred her darling husband's urn into her large canvas bag. Back at the check-in desk, the lady smiled at her.

"Yes, madam, this is fine now. Have a lovely trip and I hope you will fly with us again soon."

Samantha returned her smile and headed for the hand luggage section. She braced herself as her canvas bag went through the X-ray machine. A few seconds later, she realised it was not coming down the conveyor belt. The official turned to her.

"Is this your bag, madam?"

"Yes," she replied, a slight nervousness creeping into her voice.

"I need to look inside. I have an object on my screen I don't recognise."

Sam peered over the desk and looked at the image.

"I can explain," she volunteered. "It's my late husband's ashes. He died recently, and it was his last wish to be scattered in Sorrento, where we married."

The officer turned to Sam. Compassion was etched on her face. "Oh, how sad."

Samantha's eyes filled with tears triggered by this kind woman.

"Do you have any paperwork from the undertakers, also a Death Certificate? If you have, then we can let you travel."

Sam handed over the documents and thanked the lady for her kindness. She headed for the departure lounge and the start of her husband's last journey, hugging her bag and Robbie to her heart.

MARY

Mary picked up her holiday clothes and rearranged them into piles. It was only two hours before she had to leave for the airport, and she was struggling to decide what to take.

"I must be crazy to go back to Italy after all these years." She spoke out loud to herself. "It's insane to recreate a relationship after twenty years. Maybe I should leave everything dead and buried? He's bound to be married, with kids."

Her thoughts drifted back to their love affair. '*How did it all go so wrong? And why can't I get this man out of my head*?' Reaching for a pair of elegant strappy shoes and packing clothes in her case, she popped in a photograph album of happy times spent with the man she was in love with and who haunted her thoughts every day.

Disillusionment with life had led to this rash decision. Constant travelling around the world as cabin crew for BA had been a wonderful experience. But now she was tired. Her life seemed empty and pointless. Reaching for a framed photograph of their time together, she stared into his soft brown eyes and said.

"I'm coming back to find you. It's been a long time, but I have to know if you still love me? Does your heart ache each time you think of me, or am I deluding myself? I will understand if you are happy, and I promise I won't upset your life if you are. But, my darling, I need answers for once and for all whether you still have feelings for me."

She placed the picture on top of her clothes and secured the lid; she was ready to go.

THE JOURNEY

(Il Viaggio)

The airport was filling up with early morning travellers. John sat in the airport café, a cup of black coffee in his hand. He liked his coffee strong and black; in fact, he was precise in all things in his life. People watching fascinated him, especially looking at their choice of luggage. Being a designer and manufacturer of high-quality bags, John couldn't help himself. It always surprised him when he saw what people carried, ranging from bog-standard cheap suitcases to backpacks and overfull carrier bags. It was unusual for someone to walk past him carrying a smart leather suitcase or handbag.

"Is anyone sitting here?" a voice broke into his thoughts.

"Only me," John said.

He looked at the woman in front of him. She was young and pretty. Her lovely blonde hair, fashionably cut, tumbled across her fine bone-structured cheekbones, but her pale blue eyes showed signs of sleepless nights.

"You can put your bag on this spare chair if you like?" John said. His rich, cultured voice usually made women notice him, but not this time.

"No thanks," Samantha replied, still hugging her bag to

her chest. "I'm fine. I don't want to lose it." She smiled and stirred her coffee.

"Are you travelling far?" he asked, trying to make polite conversation.

"Sorrento," she replied.

"So am I, well, Naples first. I'm heading for a business meeting to sell my range of leather goods." John prattled on. Sometimes he had a problem communicating with people, often feeling out of place. Even in his army career, he struggled with his mates, who made fun of his 'strange' ways. He knew he had OCD, but it helped him to cope with life and kept him on an even keel. In his military career, they commended him for volunteering for dangerous missions in Afghanistan. He'd killed people to save other people. Even now, nightmares haunted him. He stopped talking, sensing this beautiful young woman wasn't listening.

Samantha rose from the table and wished him good luck as she headed off towards the departure lounge. She just wanted this journey over with.

*

The flight set off on time and the passengers settled into their seats for the three-hour journey.

Eva, seated next to a woman with a small child, quickly made friends with the little boy who sat between them. It was his first flight, too. His excitement became infectious as the plane took off. Once in the air, Eva invited him to sit on her knee so they could both peer out of the window. They gazed in astonishment at the clouds, but when the plane bounced a little their smiles turned to anxiety. The fasten seat belt sign came on and the pilot reassured passengers it was only temporary turbulence owing to thunderstorms over Italy.

"The pilot said it's going to be OK," Eva reassured the little boy. "It's exciting, isn't it?"

He glanced up at her and smiled, but reached for her hand for comfort, and Eva gladly took it.

Meanwhile, Mary was relaxing and enjoying the novelty of being a passenger instead of a flight attendant. Her thoughts drifted back to work, and she reflected on what had made her disillusioned with her life. Most of the men she came into contact with were married or gay. Some married men were terrible. They didn't even try to hide the fact they had a wife and kids, they just wanted a relationship without ties, or respect, or love.

At first, it didn't bother her. Male companionship was welcome after a long flight. Someone who would spoil her with expensive gifts and evenings spent in the world's best restaurants was something she enjoyed. It felt exciting to wear beautiful clothes and be admired. To be held in their arms through the night was irresistible.

She sipped her coffee and allowed her thoughts to wander back to the day she realised her life had changed. At first, she put it down to a mid-life crisis. One of those birthdays people deny is happening. She had spent the day working and hoped no one would remember. But that didn't happen. Not with the crew she worked with. They dragged her out to a gay Night Club in New York and let their hair down dancing the night away until it was time to sober up and head to the airport and back to work.

For Mary, it had been an ordeal. It was bad enough reaching forty, but her usual exuberance for life had disappeared. She was bored with this meaningless existence, something she hadn't experienced before, and it worried her. She loved her gay colleagues. They made the long trips bearable with their light-hearted observations of life. They wore their hearts on their sleeves and never pretended to be anything other than what they were. And they treated her with respect and loved her. But disappointment with her life had crept in, and it didn't take her long to realise that it was time for a drastic change.

Franco was always there at the back of her mind. In a moment of youthful wild enthusiasm, she had decided against heading to University to study languages and instead bought a one-way ticket to Italy, choosing Sorrento because it looked warm and beautiful. Her life spent in care and foster homes, and no family to worry about, gave her freedom to make her own decisions. She packed a bag and headed off. Although she could only speak a few words of Italian, she secured a job in a travel agency and threw herself into her new life.

A few months later, she was in the office when Franco walked in. She had been busy dealing with some difficult German customers and didn't notice he was watching her. She efficiently dealt with them, her A-level German coming in handy.

He waited for her to finish and then stepped forward, speaking in German; he asked.

"Fraulein, perhaps you can also help me?"

"Of course," she said.

He starting speaking in Italian and she interrupted him, saying she was English and her Italian wasn't as fluent as her German. Not that it was a problem for him and he changed to English mid-sentence.

"My name is Franco. Is Tomaso free?"

"I'm sorry, but he is not here. Is he expecting you?"

"No, I was just passing and thought he might be available. I run boat trips to Capri and I'm always looking for tourists who want to visit the island and the Blue Grotto. You should join us? If you haven't been before, I'm sure you will like it."

She had accepted without hesitating. There was something about him that intrigued her, and she wanted to get to know him more. A few days later, she joined him for a day out and it was about to change her life. Love had struck, and there was nothing she could do to stop it.

The pilot interrupted her thoughts as he announced they would shortly arrive in Naples and to prepare for a bumpy landing, as the storm was quite bad. The fasten seat belt sign came on.

Eva clasped the little boy's hand, smiling at him and saying he would have a lot to tell his friends about this big adventure.

John, who had been going over his presentation to prepare for his meeting, put away his briefcase and fastened his seat belt, then closed his eyes.

Samantha wrapped her feet around her bag and reassured herself that Robbie was with her and she would get through this ordeal.

The flight attendant gently woke Martha from her first-class seat. She had slept most of the journey and was told it was time to prepare for landing.

*

HOTEL

GRAND ITALIA

SORRENT0

The weather, which greeted the passengers, was a total surprise. Huge thunderclouds filled the skies with flashes of lightning, illuminating the dramatic outline of Vesuvius, the iconic volcano that dominated Naples. The rain continued its torrential downpour and everywhere looked decidedly grey and gloomy.

John collected his luggage and soon his taxi was driving through some dodgy-looking streets to the address Signor Bartolino had given him. From what he could see of the area, it looked scruffy. Neglect and poverty hung in the air, made even worse by the weather. His peripheral vision alerted him to any danger.

The taxi stopped outside a run-down tenement building.

"Surely, this can't be it!" John spoke to the driver.

"Si, Si, Signor. Piazza Municipio, 28 Via Toledo."

He rang the bell and waited. A young man, who John noticed was eyeing up his watch, took him up a steep staircase. Signor Bartolino sat behind an enormous, shabby desk. He was an ugly man. A huge spaghetti-filled stomach and an unshaven face did nothing to enhance his look. The stench of stale cigar smoke hung in the air. He greeted John with a jovial smile and broken

English.

"Sit, Signor. It is my pleasure to meet you."

John declined the outstretched hand and sat upright in a hardback chair.

After showing his samples and designs, and explaining the craftsmanship involved, he sat back, waiting for a response. The offer Signor Bartolino made was insulting. How on earth could anyone make a profit dealing with this cheat of a guy? Such a time-waster! The annoyance with himself for spending money he couldn't afford on a trip to Naples added to his anger, but the website fooled him into thinking it was genuine. He felt the urge to lean over the desk and thump the obnoxious little man.

"Stop!" yelled John, as Bartolino's grubby hand touched his samples. "I have made a mistake. I'm not sure you appreciate good quality work. The offer you just made me is insulting. I will take my leave of you."

John grabbed his bags and walked out of the room. A barrage of abuse followed behind him. "Get out of my way," he yelled to the youth lurking in the shadows of the stairway.

Outside the shabby building, John peered at the rain.

What a day. He felt annoyed with himself for booking a week in an expensive hotel, thinking Bartolino may need to see him again. His heart was thumping as he glanced up and down the street. *'Where was everybody, the place was deserted?'* Naples' dirty streets were awash with water as the rain continued to gush down the road, filling the drains to overflowing. Again, the familiar fear of being watched crept in. *'I need to get out of here.'* the voice in his head yelled. Upon reaching the end of the road, he hailed a taxi.

"Railway station for Sorrento," John spoke to the driver. Then a swift argument ensued about the exorbitant cost of the taxi. John eventually agreed, so urgent was his need to get out of this city. An hour later, the train chugged along at a slow rate to Sorrento as John sat back to reflect on his day. All his hopes had been dashed, and he was drenched to the skin. Everything seemed futile as bankruptcy loomed on the horizon. His life was a mess. It wasn't just a terrible year; his whole life had been terrible.

The walk from the station didn't lift his spirits much as the downpour continued. *'I thought the Mediterranean was hot and sunny,'* he muttered to himself. *'Maybe I should cancel my booking and try and get back home. Where on earth is the hotel?'* He thought angrily. A long road, lined with orange trees, stretched in front of him. It seemed to lead to a residential area. A passing taxi came to his rescue.

*

Eva stood at the patio window, staring at the torrential rain. She hadn't bargained for this when she had planned her trip to Italy. The air was electric, lightning constantly flashing over the bay, and the thunder was so loud it was frightening. She sighed and relaxed in one of the large comfy lounge chairs. So far, she didn't regret splashing out on the extra expense to stay in such a luxurious hotel.

She looked around the lounge. It was stunning. The simple colour scheme of cream and gold enhanced the elegance and richness of the room with touches of lavender and turquoise. The wonderful floral displays impressed her. In fact, the simple arrangement of a bowl of wine-coloured wooden fruit on the coffee table made her reach out to touch them. They looked real.

"Aren't they beautiful?" the old lady spoke softly as she settled herself in a chair.

"They are lovely and so is the colour scheme of the room," Eva replied. "It's relaxing and comfortable, especially on a stormy day like this."

"Have you just arrived, my dear?" She asked the young girl. It was such a delight to chat with someone.

"Yes, this afternoon. I wasn't expecting such horrible weather, though. It's quite a shock."

"Don't worry it won't last long by tomorrow the sun will be out again. Sometimes the rain is quite a relief from the heat."

Eva smiled "My name is Eva."

"And I am Martha. It is a pleasure to meet you."

The old lady held out her manicured hand and Eva gently took it in hers, noticing how soft her skin was and how beautifully polished her nails were.

"*Posso portarti qualcose, signorina*?" inquired the waiter who had been serving guests at a nearby table.

"Oh yes, a tea please, thank you, I mean *grazie*." She answered.

"*Prego*," replied the young man.

"Would you like some tea, Martha?"

"Yes dear, that would be very nice."

The waiter bowed his head and, with a smile that would melt anyone's heart; he walked away.

"Such a nice young man," Martha whispered. "He has a beautiful face?"

"Does he, I hadn't noticed." Eva looked towards the bar, but the waiter had disappeared.

"Well, he noticed you," Martha chuckled.

A few moments later, the waiter reappeared with their drinks. Eva slowly stirred her tea. An awkward quietness prompted Martha to say something.

"Are you here on your own?"

"Yes, I am."

"On holiday?"

"Well, yes. I've just qualified from catering college. I'm taking some time out to decide what to do next."

"Oh, you are a chef, how interesting."

"Yes, although I desperately need some experience in a restaurant. I am particularly interested in Mediterranean food. It's so versatile and exciting."

Martha's face lit up with enthusiasm. "I would be

happy to introduce you to some accomplished chefs. I grew up here and know most people. I am well known myself as my father owned this hotel. When I married my English gentleman, he took me to live in London." Martha chuckled, "there was quite a lot of gossip from the locals. I was in my twenties. It took a long time for my family to accept the situation. They wanted me to marry an Italian boy and have lots of children who would carry on the family business."

"What happened, how did it work out for you in England?"

"We had a wonderful life. I loved him dearly. He totally swept me off my feet and, when he proposed, I didn't hesitate. I was helping my father run this hotel, but George, my late husband, was a surgeon and his work was in London. He was attending a conference in Rome and afterwards had driven down to this area to experience thc Amalfi Drive he had heard so much about. He stayed here, and I met him, and it wasn't long before we had fallen in love. After he had returned home, we corresponded. I missed him, I was totally miserable, and then a few months later I was walking around Piazza Tasso and there he was, just standing watching me."

"You mean he came back for you?" Eva interrupted.

"Yes, he did. He rushed over to hug me and then whispered in my ear, *'marry me?'* I thought my heart was going to explode! We married here in Italy and then I left my family to start a new life in London." Martha's face was alive with her memories. "I came back to Sorrento to visit over the years, many times."

"Did you like London?"

"Oh yes. It was 1959 and so much was happening. The war had been over for a long time and London was being rebuilt. It was exciting and the 'in' place to be. Here in Naples it was terribly poor and badly devastated by the war. There was no money to rebuild. It was so depressing. Sorrento was still beautiful, but only rich people could afford to visit. Not like now, where tourists come from all over the world."

"What a huge decision for you, Martha, to change your life and live in another country."

"Not at all. I was in love and I've always believed life is for living. Grab every opportunity you can. If it doesn't work out it is not meant to be. But I was lucky. My husband worked hard. We lived in a nice select area in the centre of London. I didn't need to work, but I got involved in our local theatre and when the building deteriorated and it looked like we were going to close, my husband bought it for me. I turned it from a struggling amateur theatre to one of London's finest. It was such fun and our friends were famous actors and musicians. I am so fortunate. My life has been wonderful. My only regret is I didn't have children." She sighed. "Che Sara, Sara."

"What has brought you back here?" Eva asked.

"Well, my George sadly passed away recently and one morning I woke up and I just knew I wanted to go back to live in my family home where I grew up. My house has sold in London and I packed my bags and here I am. After my mother died, I inherited the family's villa. I'm just waiting for my solicitor to finish the paperwork and release the keys. It's been such a long time since I've seen it, but I know it is where I want to be."

Samantha, who had been sitting behind the two women suddenly, let out a stifled sob. She turned towards Martha and in a muffled voice said.

"I'm so sorry I didn't mean to interrupt your conversation, but I couldn't help overhearing your lovely story. I do hope you find what you are looking for."

"Martha, this is Samantha. We met on the hotel bus when we came from the airport." Eva said.

"Come and join us, dear. We are just chatting and getting acquainted."

Samantha gladly joined the two women. She needed company, and it wasn't long before the conversation turned to her. She explained, without going into too many details, the story of her and Robbie getting married in Sorrento and their plans for their future together, which sadly didn't materialise. The two women listened intently. It was Martha who touched Sam's arm and softly whispered her condolences.

"How sad, my dear. You have been through so much and now you want to lay your Robbie to rest. If I can help you, please let me know. There are many secret coves and beautiful quiet locations hereabouts. I can arrange for someone to show you if you like?"

Samantha smiled and was just about to thank her when

a disturbance at the reception desk made them all turn around. A soaked and irate John was quarrelling with the manager.

"What do you mean, you haven't got my booking? I did it online and paid a deposit for a week's stay."

"Signor my apologies, we have no record of it and I'm sorry, but we are fully booked. Perhaps you have your receipt on you?"

"What!" John raised his voice as he put down his luggage and rifled through his wallet.

"Look, here it is" he ungraciously flung a piece of paper down on the desk.

The manager immediately began a heated discussion with his reception staff. Martha stood up and walked over to John.

"I am the owner and I hope you will accept my sincerest apologies for this inconvenience." She spoke to the manager in Italian, telling him to transfer John to a suite at their expense. "We hope you will accept, with our compliments, a superior room." She smiled. "I expect you will want a hot shower and rest. You seemed to have been caught in this most inclement weather."

John looked down at his wet clothes and the puddle of water that oozed over his shoes onto the highly polished floor. Calming down, he stared at the old lady. His back suddenly straightened as though he was standing to attention.

"That would be most acceptable. I am sorry for raising my voice, it has been a bad day for me." He shook her hand and then turned to the manager to apologise for his behaviour.

"Signor, the fault is on our part. Please accept our sorrow for your inconvenience."

He smiled at Martha who signalled for the bellboy to take John to his room. Thankfully, the incident was over.

*

The Hotel Grand Italia tried to provide their guests with some comfort from the storm. The waiters filled the lounge with candles as the dark clouds and thunderstorms encased the hotel.

A guest was playing romantic music at the grand piano. The chefs and kitchen staff worked overtime to provide delicious food, as the restaurant was fully booked for the evening.

After seeing his luxurious bedroom, John threw off his wet clothes and stood under the hot shower. It was heaven, and he just allowed himself to enjoy the warmth. Changing into a soft bathrobe and pouring himself a whisky from his duty-free, he walked around the room.

The view from the floor-to-ceiling window was hard to make out. A thick mist covered the hills and the rain just kept on coming. He lay on the bed and closed his eyes, trying to work out a plan. Should he head home tomorrow or stay the week and try to find other buyers? The whisky was working its magic and within a few minutes, he was asleep.

A couple of hours later, John headed for the restaurant. He had hardly eaten all day, and the thought of dinner was uppermost in his mind. The restaurant didn't open for another hour, so he made his way towards the bar.

Guests were drifting into the lounge area. After ordering a whisky, he allowed his thoughts to wander. Life had been tough lately. Everything had gone wrong after he left the army. Amanda came into his mind. He should never have married her. She'd never understood him, or even tried to help him get through his problems. After experiencing therapy for his post-traumatic stress, she had laughed at his obsessive ways and never tried to help him. He was a passionate man who loved beauty, spending hours polishing his leather goods, running his fingers over the soft calf leather. It brought him comfort, something he didn't get from his wife. She used him and tossed him aside when she got bored. He'd worked so hard to provide for her and she thanked him by leaving him for some stupid garage owner with dirty fingernails. What really hurt the most was she packed her bags with his expensive set of snakeskin leather suitcases and just left him a note. The experience had added to his anxiety and depression.

Moments later, his thoughts were interrupted.

"Gin and tonic per favour," the young woman said to the barman.

John turned and next to him stood a very attractive woman. She had dark short hair, laughing eyes and was dressed in a fabulous red lace dress that clung to her shapely body.

"Of course, Signora," the barman said.

'Grazie, and please charge it to room 318," she replied.

John wanted to get to know her. She had an air of confidence and friendliness that seemed inviting. He seriously needed companionship right now.

"Well," he spoke to her, "so much for Italian sunshine. If I'd known it was going to be like England, I would have brought an umbrella."

She turned to face him. "Don't worry, it's only temporary. Tomorrow will be hot again. You'll soon be sunbathing by the pool. Actually, I think it's quite a lovely evening. The hotel looks cosy with all the candles glowing and the smell of food is so inviting."

"Do you live here?" John responded. "You seem to know all about the weather."

She laughed. "I used to, many years ago, but I'm just visiting, hoping to catch up with old friends. I'm an air steward with British Airways and, although it is quite an exciting life, I suddenly needed to return to Sorrento. I've missed it. Are you on holiday?" She said noticing John's pale grey eyes and troubled face.

"Not really. I had a business meeting in Naples this

morning, but it was a disaster. I considered going home, but changed my mind. The thought of spending a few days relaxing seems appealing."

"What do you do?"

"Well, and please don't laugh, I design artisan leather goods, suitcases, handbags, that sort of thing from my small studio in London. I was hoping to get a big order today, but the guy I came to see was a con man!" John looked disheartened.

"That's a shame. I'm afraid there are quite a few people like that around Naples, but once you have seen the beautiful designer shops in Sorrento, I'm sure you will get some orders. The leather goods here are of outstanding quality and most tourists end up buying a leather handbag to take home."

"That's comforting to know. As soon as this rain stops, I'll take a wander around. My name is John, by the way."

"And I am Mary." She reached out to shake his hand.

*

The lounge was full of tourists. The weather caused everyone to change their plans for visiting nearby Capri or the Amalfi drive. Some guests had ventured out on the train to Pompeii only to get soaked to the skin. It was heavenly to sip a cocktail or two whilst waiting for someone else to cook dinner. A piano player in the background added to the cheerful atmosphere of being on holiday.

Martha was also enjoying the evening. After resting most of the afternoon, she received the disappointing news that there was a delay regarding the release of the keys to her villa, but her solicitor felt confident he could deliver them to her in a couple of days.

Dressing carefully for dinner she chose a salmon pink chiffon blouse with a coffee-coloured crochet skirt. Martha was a beautiful woman. Good bone structure, genes inherited from her mother, and a passion for life showed in her expressive face. She was approachable and loved it when people engaged her in conversation.

From where she was sitting, near the piano player, she could see Eva, Mary, and John chatting at the bar.

Glancing around the room, her eyes caught sight of Samantha walking across the marbled floor of the reception area. She looked so unhappy. Martha hesitated for a moment, wanting to call her over, but intuitively felt the young woman needed to be alone. It was heart breaking to see such a young person suffering alone with grief. Her shoulders were down and her entire persona screamed out, '*somebody help me.*'

Martha headed to the restaurant, which was in full preparation for the evening. Signor Miccio, the maître di, was standing by the door giving instructions to his headwaiter. He saw her coming towards him and immediately dismissed his colleague. The Signora was the owner and therefore demanded his immediate attention. He beamed his usual smile of welcome and reached out to hold her hand.

"Good Evening Madam," he spoke kindly to her. "How may I help you?"

"Ah! Signor Miccio, I have a special favour to ask you. This evening I intend to dine in the restaurant. I wonder if you would be kind enough to set the large round table near the terrace for five people. Also, there are four guests I would like you to invite them to join me. They are here on their own but I have met them and I think it would be nice to bring them together."

"Si, Signora, perhaps you could point out the guests

to me?"

"The two young women and the gentleman talking at the bar, Oh yes, and especially, the young lady sitting over by the water feature. If they have other plans, it is not a problem."

"I will do my very best Signora," and with his usual flair, he kissed her hand and escorted her back to the lounge.

The evening service was in full flow. A lovely sound of chatter and laughter filled the room as the guests discussed their day. Fortunately, Signor Miccio used his charm and grouped the four people together. They seemed quite delighted not to be eating at single tables, and were already enjoying a glass of wine. John started the conversation off by introducing himself, and it wasn't long before Martha put in an appearance

"Thank you so much for joining me this evening," she said, seating herself next to John. "I noticed you were all travelling on your own and I thought you might like some company?"

"It's a lovely idea, Martha, thank you," Eva said. "I'm not sure if you have met Mary?"

"No, I haven't but I overheard you talking to the receptionist and I have to say your Italian is very good," replied Martha.

Mary laughed. "To be honest, it is some time since I've used it. Many years ago I worked in the tourist office in town. I'm surprised how quickly it is coming back to me. It is a lovely language, and it's making me feel at home again."

Martha smiled and turning to John said, "and how is your visit going? I hope you are comfortable in your room?"

"Yes, I am. I'm still rather embarrassed by my behaviour this afternoon, but it was a shock to think I hadn't got a bed for the night."

"I've had a somewhat disappointing day myself." Martha smiled. "I was expecting to receive the keys to my family's villa, but there is some delay in releasing them and they won't be ready for a couple of days. I was hoping to see what state it is in so I can move there to live."

"That sounds exciting," John said.

"I hope so. It has been quite a few years since I've seen

it. I'm sure it must be neglected. My intention is to bring some love back into the old house."

"Who is going with you, Martha? Would you like some company?" Eva asked.

"Well I was planning on going by myself, but it would be wonderful if you wanted to come along. Are you sure I won't be interrupting your holiday?"

"Not at all, I'd prefer to visit a real Italian villa than lie in the sun all day."

"If it is all right with you Martha, I'd love to come," Samantha said.

"Me too" interrupted Mary.

"And me," John said, not wanting to miss a unique opportunity.

"How wonderful, it would be so helpful to have your advice." Martha looked delighted.

By the end of the evening, the group were relaxing in each other's company. Samantha, in particular, was quiet but she enjoyed the banter between the others and was looking forward to being part of a group of people. She needed desperately to avoid isolation and to have a normal life.

SORRENTO

Loved by all for centuries, Sorrento, a coastal town perfectly situated with a sharp peninsular and a softly curved bay majestically dominated by Mount Vesuvius, is a place of beauty and romance.

Its grand buildings and busy market streets display richness and prosperity but are shared by the working Neapolitans and visitors from all over the world who congregate to enjoy a *buona passeggiata* up and down the main streets. Artisans are eager to show their hand-carved, inlaid furniture and shoemakers making glittery sandals while you wait, all adds, to the relaxed atmosphere.

The sounds and smells of Sorrento get inside your head. It's noisy and full of life. People love to mingle whether they are dressed for a concert or out for a pizza or maybe just people watching. This is the place to be and be seen.

Yesterday was a complete washout, but the early morning brought vivid rays of brilliant sunshine. Martha, sitting on her balcony in her private quarters, watched the sunrise over the sea.

Shrouded in a shawl to keep her warm and protected

by the early morning cool air, she reflected on how much Italy meant to her. The fragrance of the flowers rising from the garden below and the beautiful morning light was spell bounding. She needed little sleep these days. Knowing her life was drawing to a close didn't worry her; instead, it increased her desire to enjoy every moment. Death was inevitable, but she wasn't in a hurry to leave this world. Since she was a small child, she was aware of the colours and beauty surrounding her. It helped to have been born in a country of sunshine and art, although her years spent in London had captured her soul, the relentless rainy days also brought comfort and cosiness into her world. Summer holidays spent in Cornwall, with the gentle silver mists of early morning floating over the estuary and the boats moored up for a night's rest sent a chill down her spine of ghostly images of a lost world.

Now the day was approaching for her to visit the villa and to decide whether this was where she wanted to spend her remaining time on this earth. In her heart, this was what she wanted, and the anticipation of seeing the lovely home again filled her with excitement.

A knock at the door and she was back to reality, as she let the waiter in with her breakfast tray. Settling back to enjoy the simple delights of hot coffee and croissants, a smile of contentment flickered across her face. It had been a delight yesterday to meet such wonderful young people and to bring them together. Her spirits were lifted, but she sensed each one of them had problems.

*

Breakfast was being served, and the waiters dressed in their light grey uniforms were busily attending to the needs of their guests. In the kitchen, the chefs shouted orders while preparing for lunch. Pasta, bread, and mouth-watering desserts were the order of the day. The Maître Di was at his desk preparing the day's menu and discussing, with his head chef how they would display the Italian food festival arranged for the evening. Combined with live music, they were expecting a full restaurant.

Signor Miccio was a small, round man with a twinkle in his eyes. He had been the inspiration in the restaurant for many years. His operatic voice and bubbly personality guaranteed guests returned year after year. They were delighted to be serenaded at dinner when he gave an impromptu singing performance of Neapolitan love songs to rich elderly female guests. He loved women; he loved life, and he loved his job. At this moment, he was arguing passionately with his chef. He also loved a good argument.

Samantha entered the dining room. She'd slept well. It was the first time since Robbie's death that confused dreams hadn't disturbed her. It had been fun being part of a group at dinner last night. She had showered and put on the bright orange dress that Robbie always said complimented her lovely figure. Her blond hair fell into long, soft strands over her shoulders. She could feel her confidence returning and was ready to cope with the world again.

After ordering coffee and a continental breakfast she sat back to watch people passing by the terrace restaurant. How wonderful to feel the warmth of the sun so early in the morning. Perhaps today was the day when she could cope with a walk around the familiar town.

She headed down towards the Cloisters. Surely there

must be a suitable place near the bougainvillea and roses where she could scatter Robbie's ashes without being seen? He'd loved the ancient arches and peaceful atmosphere, and it had been a perfect choice for their wedding. A ceremony was taking place and not wanting to intrude, she sat at a bar in the municipal gardens close by. She ordered a long cool drink and gazed at the sea. A short while later, the wedding party emerged and everyone gathered around for photographs. The young bride looked so pretty in a long white chiffon dress with embroidered flowers on the bodice in pastel colours. Her flowers matched the design on her dress. Her husband wore a cream linen suit, and the guests were in a mixture of bright colours. Everyone was laughing and taking photographs. The couple looked relaxed and happy. Then another wedding party arrived. *'They must have come from the church,'* Sam thought to herself. The contrast to the first couple was quite startling. The guests all wore black designer clothes, including the groom who wore an Armani suit. The bride was stunningly beautiful, with her black hair elegantly swept off her face and tied in a chignon at the base of her neck. A brilliant white satin

59

dress fitted tightly over her slim body, enhancing the designer look. The detail at the back of the dress had tiny pearl buttons going from the top of the dress to the hem. So simple, yet totally sophisticated.

Samantha noticed a difference between the two couples. The Italian bride's expression was sullen and moody, whereas the English girl smiled radiantly. Sam knew which wedding she preferred. After the photographs were taken, the two groups moved away. Their memories recorded for years to come.

She watched as the Italian family headed for a horse and carriage whilst the English couple, still laughing, walked hand in hand with their guests through the gardens and down the cobbled streets to a small Italian restaurant.

Sam sighed. Painful memories of her own wedding to Robbie flooded her mind. They had married in the same place and had photographs taken with the view in the background. Their close friends and family had travelled to join in the celebrations and to be part of their treasured memory.

The gardens become quiet now as the wedding parties

moved on. A few tourists walked by, couples holding hands. Small children ran around enjoying themselves. She was glimpsing the future she would never have. A lump came into her throat. The hurt and pain were so intense. She stayed a while longer, just gazing into the distance, trying to calm her emotions down.

'*Maybe the Cloisters is not the right place.*' Sam thought to herself as she walked around the old streets, ending up in Piazza Tasso. Already the sun had a lot of heat in it, and she was becoming thirsty. Finding an empty table at the Fauna Bar, Sam ordered an iced tea. She needed to be around noise and people. On the edge of an emotional journey, she was struggling to know how to cope with it all. A waiter hovered close to her. Her thoughts were far away. Memories of Robbie on their honeymoon again flooded back. She began reliving every moment. They'd sat at this café, at this very table. She could sense him sitting by her side.

"Sam, look over there have you ever seen anything like it?" he had said.

Her eyes followed his gaze, and she saw in front of her a young man riding a motorbike and clinging to him was an old lady, complete with a crash helmet and walking stick.

"Only in Italy," she laughed.

He reached for her hand and held it. "I love this place. It's crazy, beautiful, and annoying all at the same time. I still can't get over turning the tap on in the bathroom this morning and it came off in my hand!"

She remembered how he had become drenched and in desperation balanced a pot from the side table, over the tap to stop the room from flooding.

"I love it too, Robbie. I'm having the most amazing time. I shall remember this moment for as long as I live. You and me watching the world go by and knowing we have our entire life ahead of us. This will always be our special place."

He leaned over and kissed her lips.

The spell was broken as the waiter tried to catch her attention. "Signora, perhaps you would like an apéritif or some pasta for lunch?"

The memory disappeared from her thoughts, and she came back to reality and life without Robbie. She clutched her bag, but it didn't contain Robbie's ashes ....

they were next to her pillow in the hotel.

"No grazie." For a moment, her thoughts and reality confused her. She paid for her drink, deciding to retrace the walk she and Robbie had taken.

She headed down the cobbled market street in search of rekindling her memories. Her footsteps led her to the old town of Sorrento down winding cobbled pathways and passing the traditional houses. Women were shouting to each other as they hung their washing out. It was such a normal sound, away from the hustle and bustle of the tourist areas. She remembered how much they had loved this area.

"One day I will buy one of those old fishermen's cottages and turn it into a palace, and we will live here together until we get old and wrinkly. Each night we will sit on our balcony and watch the sun settle over the sea as we eat our pasta that you have so lovingly cooked for me." Robbie had said.

She had laughed out loud.

"Robbie, you are such a romantic and I hate to bring you back to reality but this time next week you will be standing in front of a class of 14-year-olds teaching them

mathematics and I will be back to nursing. This will all be a distant dream."

"It will never be a dream, Sam. This is what life should be. You and me together enjoying this wonderful day drawing to a close and knowing tomorrow the sun will rise again over the sea and all will be well. Don't think about home, this is home now at this moment forever."

They'd lingered for a while longer and arm in arm walked back to their hotel. The windows were wide open, letting in cooler air as they passionately enjoyed the pleasure their bodies freely expressed. Afterward, lying entwined in each other's arms, they'd slept as though as one person. But they would never be a couple again. She was alone. He'd left her to live her life without him. It wasn't his fault; she knew that. Thoughts of the awful time of his suffering as he dealt with the treatments the hospital used to save his life. His beautiful face was wracked with pain, his once fit and healthy body shrinking in front of her. Oh, it wasn't fair on him or her. She was angry at the cruelty of illness. Why had he died? There were moments when she wanted to follow him, but she knew that it would bring even more pain to their families. There was no choice but to carry on living. In her heart, she knew he would never have left her. She tried to feel his presence near her, but he had gone. Once more everything was empty, just numbness. She headed back to the hotel alone.

*

Eva had also woken early after a restless night. The receptionist had given instructions on where to find Marina Grande, the old fishing village. It was a twenty-minute walk down steep cobbled streets, past old houses. At any other time, she would have dawdled savouring the calmness and the magnificent views, but she was eager to find the address her mother had written on the letter to her father.

Sometime later, Eva was standing outside the old house in the tiny fishing village. This had to be the address. She glanced around; everyone seemed to be going about their business, opening up shops for the day's onslaught of tourists. She felt at a loss, not knowing what to do next. How could she knock at the door and say to whoever opened it, '*do you know my father?*'

On impulse, she headed for a coffee bar just to sit and watch the house to see if anyone came in or out. She ordered a fresh fruit juice and settled down to see what fate had in store for her. It wasn't long before someone walked by who Eva recognised. It was Mary from the hotel.

"Hi, fancy seeing you down here. Can I join you?" Mary asked.

"Of course," Eva answered brightly, pleased to see a friendly face.

Mary looked around. "I love this part of town. Twenty years ago, this used to be my favourite place when I lived here. In those days it was a real fishing village, not like now, it's quite touristy isn't it?"

Eva suddenly cheered up.

"You used to live here?" she said, trying not to get too excited.

"Yes, I rented a small apartment on the main square, but if I had a spare few hours, I would often wander down here. It is so traditional, I love it." Mary looked around her wistfully gazing at the beach and sea as it gently lapped against the shore.

"Mary, please help me. Do you recognise this man?"

She passed a faded photograph towards her. "It was taken over 20 years ago. It's not very clear."

Mary stared at the face of the man who had been in her thoughts every day for years.

"Yes, his name is Franco, but why are you asking?" she queried.

"I think he's my father," Eva replied softly.

"Your father?" Mary was visibly shocked.

"Yes, after my mother died, I found a letter and this photograph in a box my mother had kept hidden in her wardrobe. She had written it after finding out she was pregnant. For some reason, it was never posted. It was a tremendous shock, I was led to believe my step-father was my actual father, but this has changed everything."

Eva passed the letter to Mary for her to read.

My dearest Franco,

It is difficult for me to write these words, but you need to be told what has happened since I returned home.

Saying goodbye to you was so hard. I cried for weeks at the thought of never seeing your face again. We had such a wonderful time, and I longed for the day when you joined me here in England. But you never arrived or wrote to me as you had promised.

People have told me it's only a holiday romance, but it was more than that. You led me to believe you felt the same way.

Franco, I have some news for you, and I don't know what your reaction will be, but you need to know that I am pregnant. My baby, our baby, is due in March., I feel so lost and alone. Please contact me when you receive this letter.

With all my love

Diana

Mary handed the letter back. There was no way she could tell her that Franco was the person she was also looking for.

"Oh, Eva, what a sad letter, your poor mother. Something must have changed her mind about sending it. I wonder what?"

"I have no idea, maybe if I can find him he will be able to answer some questions. To be honest, I'm not sure what to do. It's all been a bit of a shock to me. You said you knew him, Mary, do you think he may still live around here? The address on the envelope is for the house over there, but I haven't yet plucked up the courage to knock at the door."

Mary glanced towards the house. It had been many years since she had seen it but it still looked the same. This was the reason why she had come here today to find Franco, but the news she had just received changed all of that.

"As far as I remember, his parents lived there." Mary pointed to one of the old buildings. "His father was a fisherman. He owned a couple of boats. Do you want me to ask the lady in the coffee bar if she knows him?"

"Oh yes please, here take the photograph."

"I won't be a minute." Mary headed off toward the café, her mind in a total whirl.

"Mi scusi signora, ti capita di conoscere quest'uomo?" (Excuse me, Ma'am, do you know this man?) She asked the elderly lady.

"Sì, è Franco, ma non è qui, è in America a trovare suo fratello." (Yes, it's Franco, but he's not here, he's in

America to visit his brother.)

"Davvero, sai quando tornerà?" (Really, when will he return?)

"Mi dispiace non lo so." She smiled. (I'm sorry I do not know)

"sembra così giovane." (he looks so young.)

"Sì, è una vecchia fotografia. grazie per l'aiuto." (Yes, it's an old photograph. Thank you for your help.)

She returned to Eva, who was waiting anxiously for news.

"Did she recognise him?"

"Yes, straight away, even though she said he looks much younger. He is not here. Apparently, he is visiting his brother in America and she has no idea when he will be back."

"Oh," Eva looked crestfallen. "Well, at least I have found his home and I know he still lives here."

Mary looked at the young woman; her deep brown eyes and long eyelashes stared back at her. It was like looking into Franco's eyes.

*

THE VILLA
(LA VILLA)

The following morning, they set off in the hotel bus to see Martha's family home. It wasn't too far from Sorrento, along a narrow uphill road and hidden from view by overgrown trees.

Martha stood at the entrance gate to the villa. She sighed; a memory was forming in her mind, something from a long time ago. As a little girl, she remembered skipping amongst the trees, pulling figs from the branches and splitting them with her nails, devouring every mouthful of the delicious fruit. She breathed the air, taking in the fragrance, which triggered a sudden memory of her mother's voice calling everyone to the table for lunch. Her father dropped his garden tools and made haste to the veranda. He loved his wife and would rush to respond to her call.

Martha smiled as memories of her wonderful childhood came back to her. Her mother was always singing in her mezzo-soprano voice, arias from her favourite operas. Occasionally, with her husband, they would sing Neapolitan love songs together. She remembered the adoration on her father's face as he gazed at his beautiful wife.

As she opened the gate and walked down the overgrown pathway, Martha didn't notice the ground covered with rotting oranges and lemons, or how the vines had withered and died under the searing heat. All she could see was how the sunlight danced on the yellow ochre rendered walls of the villa. The sun-drenched flaky paintwork resembled abstract artwork, and to her eyes was beautiful.

She stared at the old windows as if seeing faces laughing and waving to her. Oh, how she missed her family. They were all gone now. Only she remained, but somehow this wonderful building held the secret to her future happiness.

A hint of lavender and citrus fragrances filled the air. Martha gazed at the old villa with its pale turquoise coloured shutters hanging from their hinges. Goodness, she whispered to herself, *'it's just like me, old, lonely, and sorry for itself.'* But looking again and seeing its former beauty, it filled her heart with joy, and she made a promise to the house that she would make it beautiful again. Filled with an excitement Martha had not felt for many years, and taking a deep breath, with her head high and back straight, she said aloud to the villa, "I've come home."

Martha placed the giant key into the old rusty lock on the ancient wooden door. It wouldn't open, but John, who had been walking a distance behind her, rushed to help. With a lot of pushing, the door opened. The sunlight streaked through the cracked shutters. At first, they couldn't see anything, but their eyes soon became accustomed to the glare. In front of them lay a magnificent entrance hallway. The pale peach crumbling paintwork on the walls and a chandelier covered in cobwebs revealed the secrets to the villa. As they pulled off the dustsheets, it exposed elegant furniture as though being reborn from a lost time.

"Oh Martha, dear." Sam took the old lady's arm. "You can't stay here it needs so much work." The old lady sighed. "Samantha, please don't worry. I've lived a long time and I'm tired, but I need to be back here with my memories."

Sam glanced at the others, searching for support and seeing a look of concern on their faces.

"OK," Mary interrupted. "Let's make a list of what

needs doing. We can talk later."

The beauty of the villa emerged as they explored each room, opening the shutters and letting the full sunlight cast its brilliance through the large rooms.

Eva disappeared down the winding stone steps to the floor below. She opened a door to reveal the kitchen. It was almost in darkness, the heavy shutters blocking out most of the sunlight. With a lot of effort, she pulled and tugged until they opened. Particles of dust hovered in the bright stream of sunlight, like tiny fireflies dancing in the air.

"Wow!" she exclaimed, "Oh, how amazing is this."

In front of her lay the perfect example of an old rustic Italian kitchen. From the large oak table to the heavy wooden cabinets and saucepans hanging on the beam gave an insight into what would once have been a very busy kitchen. The stone-flagged floor was clean; in fact, the entire room looked like someone had tidied and polished it, ready for its years of sleep.

Eva headed straight for the French doors and, pulling open the rusty glass, she stepped into a wonderful terraced area, complete with an old trellis walkway with overgrown vines, and fruit trees, orange, lemons, pomegranates, and figs. To her left revealed a dead herb garden. She walked down the pathway, pulling at the overgrowth. From the garden wall, she could see the entire view of the bay of Naples stretched in front of her. Brilliant blue and green colours invaded her eyes.

Back in the kitchen, Eva wandered around. In her head, she heard the chatter from Italian women as they made their pasta for the day's meals. Oh, how she would love to work in this kitchen. It was perfect. A hint of citrus fragrances filled the air from the open doorway, and she breathed it in, relishing every moment. She opened cupboards and peered inside. Everywhere was clean. The cooking pots and pans were neatly stacked, and it seemed the kitchen was designed for entertaining many people.

If only her childhood had been like this. To have had brothers and sisters, someone to play with, and lots of parties where everyone chipped in and helped with the cooking. She had never had a proper birthday party with friends. Her childhood had been lonely. She didn't know it, but something had been missing. Her mum and stepfather were never into entertaining. The house was always quiet. No music playing, and she often spent her time alone in her bedroom playing with her dolls.

"Penny for your thoughts," John said as he joined her.

"Oh, John, what an amazing kitchen this is. I can't believe the number of pans they had. Plenty here to cook for the entire town."

"It's wonderful. I've just been upstairs? There must be at least 10 bedrooms and all are magnificent. I don't know about you, but I grew up in quite a modest little house. This is a palace."

"John," Eva whispered to him," do you think Martha will live here? It's going to be lonely with all these empty rooms and the villa needs such a lot of work."

"Yes, you are right, it does need some attention. I can understand her wanting to go back to her roots, but all the people she loved are gone. We'll have a chat with her to see what her thoughts are."

"Well, if she is looking for a cook and house-keeper, I'll volunteer. I would love to live here and work in this kitchen."

"That's an idea. My life is going nowhere and, between you and me, Eva, I feel happy in Sorrento. I hated it a couple of days ago but I get the lifestyle now and it's made me realise that living in London is hard and lonely."

"I agree. I've been wishing I had been part of an Italian family. Lots of people coming around to eat outside in the sunshine and also cooking food you've grown or picked off the trees."

They had another look around and, locking the French doors and shutters, headed upstairs. Mary and Samantha had gone outside to walk down to the sea. Martha was sitting in an armchair, taking it all in.

"There you are. How do you like my little villa? I'm excited to hear your opinion." She smiled, her face was bright with excitement, and her eyes were glowing. She was hoping the villa had entranced them.

"Martha, it's enchanting," Eva replied, and John chipped in.

"I didn't realise it was so big. You must come from a large family?"

"Of course, we are Italian. Children are everything. There are two wealthy families in Sorrento that own most of the expensive hotels, and I've been fortunate to come from one of them. I've few relatives left, having lost my brothers and sister a few years ago, but I'm sure if the word got out that I was back and planning a big party I would be overwhelmed with cousins I've never met. I'm so pleased you like it." Martha smiled.

" Where are the others?"

"They must still be looking around." John sat next to Martha. "I don't think they will be long."

Samantha and Mary were walking back towards the villa.

"Isn't it lovely," Sam said. "Look at the plasterwork, it is so old, but looks like it's been deliberately done. I wish Robbie was here, he would have loved it." She sighed, and Mary touched her arm.

"It must be difficult for you. You must miss him so much. I wish I could help, but there is nothing anyone can do to make it better."

Sam turned to her. "Thank you, I appreciate that." Changing the subject, she asked. "Have you ever been in love, Mary?"

A little taken aback by Sam's question Mary was unsure how to answer. She wasn't used to talking about herself, but felt she needed to.

"Yes, I was in love once with an Italian guy when I lived here; I presumed he felt the same. I had hoped we would get married, all the usual things, family, kids, nice house, but as soon as I realised he believed I was an English girl just looking for fun, I left and went back to England without saying goodbye. I'm sure he was fond of me, but marrying a foreigner wasn't accepted as it is now. His mother would not have approved. I was hoping to bump into him to relight the flame." She laughed, but deep down she realised this was not going to happen.

Samantha was enjoying the conversation said.

"It's strange, isn't it? We've only known each other for a couple of days, and yet we seem to have a lot in common. We are all lost not knowing where to go next with our lives."

"And Martha," Mary interrupted. "Imagine how she is feeling. To lose your life partner and suddenly you are on your own at an age when you need love. She is very brave to come back here."

"I don't like the thought of her living here on her own, do you?"

"Well, she has her memories and money, which always buys help, but I'm sure she doesn't want to live in the past. She is so vibrant and interested in people and their lives. I think she is as lonely as the rest of us."

Heading back to the villa, they chattered away about romance and love. They found the others in the sitting room. Martha asked, "What's the verdict? Do you like it?"

"It's perfect," they both agreed.

"Sam and I have been down to the beach. The view of the bay is gorgeous and there is a secluded cove with a boathouse. Does this all belong to the villa?"

"Yes, dear, it does. It is a long time since I've been down there." She chuckled. "We had a boat and often went to Positano and Capri for swimming." She smiled. "Today has been so lovely. Thank you all for coming with me. I've enjoyed it more with having you all here."

"I think I can speak for everyone, Martha. Your home is beautiful and we are all very envious!" John said.

Samantha decided now was a good time to broach the subject of how Martha was going to cope on her own.

"Now you are reacquainted with the house, is there

much that needs doing to make it a place where you want to live?" she asked.

Martha's sigh was quite audible.

"It needs work, but I can get a team of cleaners in. The re-decorating shouldn't take too long. When I first arrived, I was in a bit of a dream world. My memories are so strong I even imagined I heard my parents shouting to me. But now I've sat looking around, I'm not sure what to do. If only George was here, he would know."

Eva rushed forward and gave Martha a hug; she could see that the old lady was close to tears.

"I'll stay with you… if you want me to? I can take care of you and cook you wonderful meals."

Samantha joined in. "Me too. I love the villa. I'll help you get settled in and get a job at the local hospital."

"Don't leave me out." John said. "I could carry on my business from here and help you with the gardens."

Mary, without hesitating, added, "or me, I'm sure I could support myself by getting a job as a tourist guide."

Martha stared at each one of them. "Do you mean you would like to make this your home also? It would make me so happy. I was instinctively drawn towards you all. You are very simpatico."

"It could work. If we combine our skills, we can get the villa back into shape and there are a lot of opportunities for jobs in the area. Are we all agreed?" Mary said.

The reply was unanimous. After a final tour around, they were soon heading back to the hotel with the prospect of an exciting new future ahead of them.

*

Back in the hotel, Mary headed for the swimming pool. She needed a few moments to reflect on her impulsive decision. Was she still hoping to reconnect with Franco? Even though she was unsure if that was wise, knowing that Eva was his daughter? With him being away in America, it was a breathing space, giving her time to think of her next move. Her sudden announcement that she also wanted to live in the villa had surprised her. Did she say that because she was unhappy with her life? One thing was certain, being back in Sorrento was where she wanted to be, and living in the villa was very appealing.

She had never forgotten the love she had for the town. The idea of making this her home was exciting, and why not? With all her experience and language skills there must be work available as a tourist guide? Money wasn't a problem as her bank account was healthy. The only thing she had to do was tell her employer and flatmates she was leaving. Yes, she liked this idea. It was an opportunity and a new direction, a purpose again. She headed for the pool and dived in, enjoying the cool water as it calmed her hot body.

Meanwhile, John and Eva had walked into Sorrento. So far they had little time to explore, and they were both delighted with what they saw. John couldn't take his eyes off the boutique shops. The leather goods were exquisite and up to the standard of work that he was making.

"John, what do you think of these gorgeous bags?" Eva pointed to a window display of large handbags. "They are so practical but fun, and the price is not expensive. I think I'm going to buy one."

They stepped inside the shop, and Eva headed straight to the displays.

"I love this bright yellow one."

John picked it up and examined it. "It's excellent quality leather. You would pay a lot more in London. Go on buy it."

"I will," she said excitedly and headed for the counter.

'*Maybe I could sell my work here?*' he thought to himself as he looked around. Martha had offered to introduce him to some buyers. It wasn't beyond the realms of possibility that he could transfer his workshop to one room in the villa. That way he could support himself. Maybe this was the break he was looking for?

*

Later that evening, after dinner, which comprised more talking than eating, everyone gathered for coffee on the terrace. Relaxing in comfy chairs with the lights of the bay flickering in front of them, they made plans for their future.

"I guess we will be heading back to London on Saturday to get our jobs sorted?" John said. "I need to cancel my lease and get rid of a lot of stuff."

Sam agreed. "There is so much to consider, I don't know where to start. I must ring my parents and Robbie's mum and dad. They will be so surprised; I only came out for a week!"

"It's an exciting opportunity," Mary said as she poured the coffee. "Has anyone had any second thoughts?"

"Not me," Eva replied.

Mary spoke carefully, "I had a few doubts, but I've made my decision. It's a chance worth taking. I can't keep flying the skies, I'm ready for a change and this is it. The summer is very busy so it shouldn't be a problem getting work, but in the winter most hotels close, as the weather can be quite cool. Ah, look here comes the lady of the moment."

'Good Evening," Martha said as she joined them. "Well, I've had the afternoon to make some plans so I would like to put a proposition to you all. The villa is in quite an awful state and I need help. I've been considering how this is going to work for you and I came up with an idea."

They grouped closer together, intrigued to hear Martha's plan.

"I've been in the hospitality trade most of my life, so I know the industry well and I was considering turning part of the villa into an outdoor restaurant, with terracing overlooking the bay? If Eva agrees, I would be more than happy to let her take the lead in the kitchen. Obviously, we can discuss the finer details, like salaries, etc., but I can see it working, especially as the villa is close to Sorrento. There is always an opening for a really wonderful restaurant in a spectacular setting."

Ever practical, Mary interrupted. "It's a great idea. We need a business plan and cost it out. I'd be happy to put my savings into the project because it has the potential to be really successful."

"Mary, that is kind of you, but my dear, not at all necessary. I can finance this venture easily. I'm really interested in your reactions, especially Eva. Is it too much for you, dear? I will hire extra kitchen staff to help you."

Eva was struggling to speak. "It's an enormous challenge, but when I saw your kitchen this morning, I knew I'd love to cook in it." Tears welled up in her eyes and Sam immediately turned to hug her.

"Are you all still happy or has anyone any second thoughts?" Martha was straight to the point.

"We've been discussing it and we are all agreed," John answered. "This wonderful opportunity you are giving us is quite overwhelming."

Martha smiled, "I'm so happy to hear that John. I know it's all quite sudden, for me too. Anyway, I imagine you all have a lot to talk about so I'll say goodnight. It has been a wonderful day, but I'm tired. Too much excitement!" she laughed, "I'll say one thing though: we are now at the end of May and if I can get workmen in to decorate, etc., we could be looking at the beginning of July to open. In the winter, we can do more repairs. The bedrooms are grim, but we can decorate them and I must get the plumbing sorted and Eva, if you can let me have a list of kitchen equipment I'll get that ordered. Does this give you enough time to sort out your affairs at home?"

"We are going back as arranged on Saturday," Mary said. "We need to give notice at work, but it's good to have a date to work to and, I don't know about the rest of you, but I can't wait to come back and get started."

"I don't want to rush you. Take your time over the next few days. It is a big change for you. Anyway, I will say goodnight and enjoy your evening."

After Martha had gone to bed, they looked at each other.

"It gets better. What a great idea. A restaurant. Wow, we need to pool our talents and come up with a definite plan." Mary said.

"Would anyone like a walk into Sorrento?" John suggested. "I'd like to see it at night time."

"Brilliant idea," Mary said. "Come on, guys, let's see what is going on in town."

They all agreed, and fifteen minutes later, they met in the foyer. The walk around Sorrento was just what they needed. Piazza Tasso, the meeting place, was alive with people. Eva kept stopping at most of the restaurants to photograph their menus for ideas.

Sam and Mary wandered in and out of the boutiques admiring the clothes.

"Anyone fancy a drink? The Foreigner's club is a good place, it has fabulous views." Mary suggested.

"Great, lead the way." John said.

They were soon ordering cocktails and sat watching as the moon rose over the bay, sending silver sparkles on the water. A small group of musicians played Latin songs and they relaxed, taking in the beautiful evening.

Walking back to the hotel in the early hours, arm in arm, they couldn't stop laughing at Mary, who had been chatting to the musicians. She was sure they would be the perfect group for the opening night of the restaurant.

*

The week passed quickly. Their days were spent sunbathing and boat trips to Capri and Positano. Never having experienced the area before, Eva could not control her excitement.

"I cannot believe this," she cried, as she leaned over the side of the boat to take photographs of the picturesque houses built on the cliff side. The brilliant blue sky and explosion of colour, was so exciting. Never in her life had she seen anything as beautiful as Positano.

Mary had been standing staring at the giant hole at the top of the mountainside. Memories of her last dinner with Franco came flooding back to her. The tiny village of Montepertuso perched high in the sky overlooking Positano, held a special place in her heart.

They enjoyed a leisurely lunch in a restaurant on the beach.

"Somebody pinch me!" Eva said. "Is this real? I've only ever been to Margate, and that was for the day. I never knew such beautiful places existed. This must be what heaven is like."

Mary laughed. "This is just the start, Eva. There are so many towns to visit. Wait until you see the blue grotto in Capri. That will seal the deal on whether this is to be your home forever."

Wandering around the tiny streets and looking into the boutique windows they couldn't resist buying summer dresses and swimwear. As for John, he disappeared, exploring the leather shops. The design and quality of the goods on offer were really impressive, and he left his contact details in the hope they would contact him for the chance to view his work.

The day lingered, becoming very special to everyone. They were bonding together and enjoying each other's company. Soon it was time to head back to the boat and the glorious trip back to Sorrento.

"When we have time, we will have to do the Amalfi drive," Mary said. "Positano from high up is amazing. It's truly stunning and the coastal road with all the bends takes your breath away."

"I can't wait to see more. I really don't want to go back to England, even for a short time," Eva said.

"Don't worry we will soon return and our time will be so busy getting this project up and running," John replied. "This is our future and a chance to have a brilliant life."

*

ENGLAND
(Inghilterra)

The days flew by and soon it was time to go back home. Arriving in England to wind and rain, they said their goodbyes to each other and promised to keep in touch.

Eva opened her front door. Everything looked the same as when she had left it only a week ago. The only difference was she had changed. Quickly switching on the heating to take the chill off the cold house, she made a cup of tea and sat by the fire. The unpacking could wait until later. It was more important to get her thoughts in order.

It had been a whirlwind few days. Finding where her father lived had been amazing, but disappointing to discover he was in America. There was always a chance he would come back and perhaps the opportunity would arise to meet him. Then to meet Martha and the others and be given a chance to fulfil her dream of running a restaurant was just incredible. It was all going so well and she couldn't wait to start her new life, but first, she had to get rid of the old one. Looking around her sitting room at the bits of furniture that had made up the early part of her life, she couldn't wait to dispose of it all.

"I think I will put the house in the hands of an estate

agent tomorrow and arrange an auction sale of the furniture." She said aloud to herself. *"There is nothing I want to keep, except for a few photographs and personal things."*

Her thoughts turned to her mother. *"I'm sorry, mum, it didn't turn out the way you wanted your life to go. I now understand how you must have felt when you went to Sorrento."* Sadness overwhelmed her. If only her mother had talked to her. How different their relationship could have been. *'Why didn't you tell me about him? It was cruel of you.'* But her mother wasn't there to listen to her daughter. Eva realised it didn't serve any purpose to think about what might have been. *'It's this house and the memories which are making me sad. I need to get rid of it as soon as possible and get back to my new life.'*

A few hours later, Eva's mobile phone rang.

"Hi Eva, it's me, Mary. How are you?"

"Oh hi, it's lovely to hear a friendly voice. I can't wait to get back to Italy. What about you? Is that music I can hear?"

"Yes, it is. I'm continuing the mood from our holiday. There is not much for me to do. I'm meeting my boss on

Monday to discuss when I can leave. My flatmates have someone in mind for my room, so that's good and I just need to sort a few things. I was wondering if you would like to meet in town next Saturday? Maybe we could go shopping and have lunch somewhere? Make a day of it."

"I would love that. It's so quiet here and lonely."

"Just keep focussed and busy. The time will soon fly and we'll be back before we know it. I'll ring you later in the week. In fact, I'll ring Sam and John to see if they want to join us."

"Great, thanks, Mary. I really appreciate your call."

Eva put the phone down, and a feeling of happiness came over her.

Mary was such an interesting person. It was nice to know she had made a good friend.

Meanwhile, Mary was wondering how she felt about Eva, knowing she was Franco's daughter? She couldn't deny it had been a shock, but she liked this young woman who, by the sounds of it, had not had the best start in life–a bit like herself. And they already had a connection… Franco!

*

A few days later, they met in Camden Town, and much to their delight; the weather had changed to a mini heat wave.

Samantha looked stunning in a black cotton jumpsuit. Her long, natural blonde hair flowed loosely over her shoulders.

"Wow! Look at you," Mary said, as they gave each other a hug. "I love your outfit."

"Thank you," she laughed, "it's so nice to see you Mary and I like your dress. Red is definitely your colour."

"Oh, look, here comes Eva. Who would know she is about to become a chef in a top restaurant, she is so young."

"Eva, we are over here," Mary yelled.

"Hi, hope you haven't been waiting long."

"No, we've just arrived. John can't make it. He sends his apologies, but he's got someone coming to discuss taking over his lease."

"That's a shame, but good for him."

"Come on girls, I've booked a table in an Italian restaurant by the river." Mary led the way. They chose a table overlooking the water and ordered a bottle of Prosecco.

"How did your family take your news, Sam?" Eva asked kindly.

"They assumed I was joking!" Samantha laughed. "But they soon came round when they saw how much happier I looked, and they got really excited when I told them about the villa. They said it is just what I need. Robbie's parents gave me their blessing and his mum cried, which set me off." Sam paused as she took a sip of wine. "My brother has volunteered to take care of the sale of my house and arrange for some of my furniture to be sent over. I've been to the hospital, and they said I could leave now. My boss was very understanding. I was quite overwhelmed."

"Gosh, you've been busy. So, no second thoughts?" Eva said.

"None. In fact, I can't wait to get back. I'll miss my family, but I'm sure they will come over and visit me. What about you two? Are you both organised?"

"I've got the house listed with an agent who will show people around, and I'm almost ready to go. What about you, Mary?"

"Well, my boss has been great and, as I have some holidays due to me, I'm finishing work next Friday. So I'm ready. Do you want me to arrange flights? I was figuring two weeks from today. What do you think?""The sooner the better for me," Eva said. "Mum's house is lonely, but I've not wasted time. I've so many ideas for menus and I've been cooking and experimenting. Trouble is, there is nobody to eat it!"

"That date is fine for me, too. I need to get back. I've left Robbie's ashes with Martha and I've had time to reflect and I'm very positive about the future."

"Well, that's agreed. I'll check with John to see if it suits him and I'll get back to you all. Anyone fancy another glass before we hit Camden market? We need to do some serious clothes shopping."

*

Martha had also been busy. She arranged a meeting with the hotel management to help with organising her new project. A team was set up to get on with the renovations. Signor Miccio insisted on accompanying her to the villa. He was eager to give his opinion, as restaurants were his speciality. Martha was delighted, and they were soon driving the short distance into the hills to her new home.

"Mamma Mia, look at this place." Speaking in his Neapolitan dialect, he continued. "Signora, I'm sure it won't take long to clear the overgrowth and general repair work, but my dear lady, it is magnificent."

They had walked through the vineyard and fruit trees and were now standing gazing up at the house.

"Come, let me show you the terrace. It's perfect for outdoor dining." Martha said.

Signor Miccio walked around humming to himself, his arms waving theatrically. "An awning or terracing to keep the shade off the clients when the weather is not so kind would be a good idea. Perhaps a roof terrace might work with vines growing over to give atmosphere? The view is simply stunning. I did not know the bay was so visible from here."

"My grandfather bought the land to build a house for his new wife. Over the years, he extended, and it became our much-loved family home. I'm sorry to see it neglected. What I want to do is give it a new lease of life."

"That can easily be achieved, Signora. I envy your passion."

"Yes, I'm going to enjoy every moment. Now let me show you the kitchen. I need your expert advice." They moved slowly inside, unaware of a stranger watching them from behind the trees. He didn't like people. '*Who were they? And how was he going to make them go away?*' He moved closer to the building.

"Now this kitchen is perfect," Signor Miccio announced in a loud voice, which echoed around the empty room. "It is such a good size and can accommodate two or three chefs easily. I love the way the doors lead directly out onto the terrace. The guests can be part of what is happening in the kitchen. It adds a lot to the atmosphere."

"Who is that?" Martha interrupted. "A person is looking through the window!" They both turned,

101

expecting someone to walk through the door.

"I don't think there is anyone there, Signora."

"That's strange. I definitely saw a face looking in at us."

"Perhaps it was just a trick of the light."

Martha agreed, but she felt uneasy, although she wasn't sure why.

Signor Miccio continued. "My dear Signora, you have a wonderful opportunity to create a stunning restaurant with excellent food and music. It is the perfect setting for success. I would love to offer my services but, as you know, I could not possibly leave your hotel. I love it too much. I hope though that I can help you when I have time off and can be of service to you."

"I would gladly appreciate your help and I value your advice. I know the hotel wouldn't be as popular as it is if it hadn't been for your dedication. Would you like to continue the tour? I am really enjoying hearing your thoughts," she said, smiling. The face at the window had disappeared from her mind.

*

THE OPENING
(L'APERTURA)

The villa was preparing for the opening night. All the repair work had been completed to the ground floor areas, which had been painted and looked fresh and inviting.

John worked hard cutting back the overgrowth whilst keeping a rural natural feel to the gardens. He cleared the driveway of rotting fruit and bushes, so diners would be greeted with an unobstructed view of the villa as they drove up the long drive.

The old oak doors were open, enticing guests to enter the vast reception area, with its glittering chandelier casting light over the marble floor. An archway with strings of tiny white lights led guests through to the dining area. Outside, the wrought-iron terrace looked inviting. Yellow fairy lights, entwined in the lemon trees, gave splendour and elegance. Black wrought iron dining tables covered with cream tablecloths and matching chairs with yellow cushions completed the look. Each table displayed a bowl of lemons as a centrepiece. Large candleholders dotted around the terrace added to the atmosphere. Inside the kitchen, the French doors were left wide open. Eva decided it would be nice for diners to step inside the kitchen and be part of the dining experience. She was hoping to create an impression of informality.

Mary and Samantha had chosen the colour scheme and crockery, and they were happy to wait on tables and get a good vibe going. Martha had taken on extra staff to help. For Eva, she hired a young Danish man as her sous chef. His name was Henrik, and he had impressed Martha with his qualifications and calm personality. After much deliberation, everyone agreed on black barista uniforms, which were very trendy in London. Their long smart aprons tied at the back and with crisp lemon coloured sleeveless blouses with black trousers looked very professional. They dressed the kitchen staff the same. John chose a black suit and white shirt and took the role of front of house welcoming the diners and taking drink orders. Mary and Samantha waited on the tables with extreme professionalism and a cheerful demeanour. Soft romantic music playing in the background, together with the glittering lights from the Bay of Naples, added a romantic feel to the restaurant.

Martha had invited, owners of some of the largest

hotels around. She took time dressing for the evening and chose one of the vintage dresses and jewellery George had bought her. Glancing around at the full tables, she was delighted to see everyone enjoying themselves. Closing her eyes and taking in the perfume of orange blossom and white jasmine, which surrounded her table, she sighed with contentment.

For the first time since George's death, she felt calm and happy. Coming back to her roots had been the right thing to do. She silently thanked her husband for keeping watch over her and for bringing into her life the four young people who had made all this possible. As the evening wore on, Martha was becoming overwhelmed with tiredness and she made her excuses and headed for bed around one in the morning.

Signor Miccio was sitting in the corner of the kitchen, his feet in a bowl of cool water to take away the throbbing, but nothing could wipe the smile of success off his face. As soon as the last guests had departed, an enormous cheer went around the kitchen. Lots of high fives and clapping as the staff took a breather and John popped champagne bottles.

Eva knocked at Martha's door the following morning. She was carrying a tray of warm croissants, fresh fruit, and coffee. A copy of the morning paper lay next to a small spray of flowers from the garden.

"Morning Martha," she said. She could see the old lady was up and dressed and looking refreshed.

"I wondered if you might like some breakfast. How are you today?"

"Oh, my dear, please come in. I feel wonderful. I must confess I was so tired last night, mainly with excitement and emotion, but I slept well and can't wait to do it all over again tonight. Come sit beside me for a moment and tell me how you enjoyed the evening."

Eva sat on the edge of the bed and, with a genuine need for reassurance, she held Martha's hand and whispered.

"Tell me what you think? That matters the most to me."

"It was one of the most special nights of my life," Martha replied. "To see my lovely villa reborn filled with guests enjoying your delicious food. The atmosphere was just perfect, and the compliments were never-ending. Did you notice the elderly gentleman sitting by himself? I remembered him straight away. The last time I saw him, he was about 20 years old. We spent a long time chatting. He's going to call in later and, we are going to reminisce about old times."

Martha hesitated; a sudden cough caught her in mid-sentence.

Eva poured the coffee and, a few minutes later, Martha continued.

"He married an old school friend of mine, Angelina. Sadly, she passed away a few years ago, but they had six children. Can you believe it? When I was at school, I had my eye on him, such a beautiful looking boy. Goodness, if we had married, just think how different my life would have been?" The thought made her smile. "Although no one could come up to my George."

"I am so pleased you enjoyed the evening. It means the world to me. Well, I'd better get on Martha. So much to do before the next service."

"Oh, yes, dear. Thank you, last night was perfect.

*

Time passed quickly. The restaurant was a big talking point in Sorrento. It didn't take long for word to get around about a young English girl running an Italian restaurant. Tourists and local business people quickly turned up to see for themselves, and they were impressed.

As the restaurant became popular, Martha insisted on changing the opening hours. She decided they should only open for evening service six nights a week. Closing all day on Mondays would give everyone a break, and only opening for lunch on Friday and the weekend. This idea delighted everyone, especially John, who approached Martha with his thoughts on getting expert advice to get the vineyard and vegetable gardens up and running.

"I agree, John, to have our own produce would be something special," Martha said as they sat together, enjoying the late afternoon sun.

"Let me know what you need to get it started. Money is not a problem. I'm more than happy to fund it all if it helps improve the restaurant."

John smiled, discovering this beautiful place at a time in his life when he was miserable had meant everything to him. For the first time in many years, he was contented, although his night terrors were still causing him anxiety. He knew he needed to focus on a project, something he loved, and the villa was it. Surely his mental health would improve.

As for his luggage business, he still wanted to work with his hands again. It had a calming effect on him. He thought he could make the beautiful leather sandals that were so popular here and perhaps even open a craft village in the villa grounds – even a space for artists to come and paint and a cookery school for Eva. There were so many exciting possibilities.

"John, you are miles away. What are you thinking?" Martha interrupted his thoughts.

"Oh, I was just dreaming." He smiled and touched the old lady's hand.

"Have you any thoughts, John?"

He hesitated before telling Martha about his ideas for the villa.

"Oh John, how wonderful. A craft village, oh, and what about an open-air theatre with singing?" Martha leaned back in the swing seat. "Yes, and I'll dedicate it to my George. The possibilities are endless."

As they were speaking, a van drove up into the courtyard.

"John, there is a delivery for you." A shout came from the kitchen.

"Excuse me, Martha, I'll just see what it is." John headed for the courtyard.

"Oh wow! It's my equipment from London." A huge smile spread across his face.

The driver lowered it down with his small forklift and asked where John wanted it. He had already cleared a small room next to the kitchen in preparation.

"If you would like to follow me. Grazie," he said to the driver as he handed him a good tip. "Come and see, guys. I'm taking orders for handbags for you all." He was so pleased. If he only did it as a hobby, it would be great to shut himself away and enjoy his craft. The delivery of the machinery had made his day.

*

Eva opened the oven door and allowed the smell of baked rolls and croissants to escape into the kitchen.

John was making everyone coffee, and the table was set outside in the early morning warmth for a continental breakfast.

"What are you doing with your day off, John?" asked Samantha as she mixed yogurt into her bowl of fresh fruit.

"I've got it all planned. After breakfast, I am going to unload my machinery and set it up. I can't wait to get my hands on a piece of leather and start creating something!"

"Sounds great. Don't forget the new handbag you promised to make me."

"Don't worry, you won't be disappointed."

"What about you, Eva? Have you any plans for your day off?"

"No, not really."

"How about a shopping trip to Sorrento? It's ages since we've been. We could take the bus down and walk back."

"Yes, that's a great idea. I need a few things. I'll tell Mary. Let's have lunch somewhere, make a day of it?"

A few hours later, the three of them were walking around the town, enjoying their well-earned day off.

Strolling down the busy streets, Mary stopped outside a jewellery shop. Something had caught her eye.

"I love this necklace, it's gorgeous."

"It is quite unusual. Looks like it's made of silver." Sam replied.

"I'm just going to pop in and see how much it is." Mary soon made her purchase. The necklace was a delicate silver cross with an unusual filigree design, and she placed it around her neck.

They wandered around the busy streets and decided on lunch at the Fauno Bar, choosing melanzane parmigiana and a bottle of wine from the menu.

"Do we really live here?" Eva said as she enjoyed watching the tourists mingling around. "It seems like a wonderful dream."

"I think it must have been fate when we all came together, and especially when Martha came into our lives." Mary took another sip of the wine as she continued. "Just imagine, I would still be doing the boring run from London to New York right at this moment."

Sam laughed. "You poor thing. Sounds like it was a

113

great life."

"It was, to begin with, but after a few years it became tedious and I could see the future was just going to be the same routine."

"Well, I loved my job as a nurse. It was rewarding. Maybe I'll go back to it one day, but at the moment I am so relaxed and content for the first time in ages."

"Yes," Mary agreed. "I'm concerned about John, though. He doesn't talk about himself much and, I don't know about you guys, but have you seen how he keeps looking behind him as though someone is following him?"

"I have," Sam replied. "He told me he is recovering from post-traumatic stress disorder from his army days. We had quite a chat about it. He's seen some terrible things, and then his wife left him for someone else. He came home one day and found a note on the kitchen table."

"Poor John, crikey, he has been through a lot. No wonder he is enjoying living here. This change will do him good." Eva reached for the bottle of wine and topped everyone up.

"Shall we just finish this and then make tracks while we can still stand? It's a long way back up the hill."

They all agreed and soon set off on the walk back, oblivious to the fact they were being followed. The stranger had been stalking them ever since they had moved into the villa. Hidden out of sight in the shadow of a doorway, he watched as they entered the jewellery shop. When he saw the jeweller take the necklace out of the window, he had become agitated and angry. He noticed that Mary was wearing the delicate filigree cross around her neck. She had no right to wear the beautiful piece. It was his, and he was going to get it back. They were unaware of his presence as laughing, and with their arms draped around each other; they started the leisurely stroll up the winding road to the villa. It had been a wonderful day.

*

Samantha woke with a jolt. It wasn't a nightmare that had disturbed her, but an overwhelming feeling that Robbie was lying next to her. For a few seconds, she believed he was. She stretched out her hand to caress his body, but he wasn't there. Stepping out of bed, she stood

115

at the window, staring out into the courtyard. Today would have been his 35th birthday. They had only been married for three years and she had been a widow for twelve months. It wasn't fair. How could such an energetic, healthy man be struck down in such a cruel way?

"Sam, it's time to let me go," the voice whispered in her ear. *"I love you, my darling, but you must move on with your life."*

"Oh Robbie, I can't let you leave me – I just can't."

"I haven't left you. I'll always be by your side for as long as you need me, but it's time to set me free."

She looked at the casket lying on her pillow and knew he was deciding for her. She must make today special, by going down to the cove and scattering the ashes on the sea. After showering and, with her spirits lifted, she dressed in a long cream coloured cotton dress, and tying her hair back into a loose knot, she was ready to go.

Samantha made her way down the rough pathway to the beach. In her arm, she clutched her canvas bag containing the casket, and some wildflowers she had picked, a large towel, and some candles and matches.

She wanted to make this an intimate and special moment for her and Robbie.

She reached the small, secluded cove with its translucent green water and placed the lit candles on the rocks. The sea was rippling on the soft sand and she laid her towel down and sat watching the soft white foam of the waves. The sounds filled her head, calming her thoughts, and as soon as the sun's rays peeped through the rocks, she knew it was time.

Slowly she removed her dress and, standing naked in the warm sunlight, she picked up the casket and waded into the water until it was waist-high. Removing the stopper, she let the fine ash sprinkle through her fingers into the sea. Speaking softly to Robbie, she declared her love and thanked him for coming into her life. There were no tears, just a sense that they were both together. Finally, she let go of the casket and swam around the little bay. As she floated on the water she said her last goodbye.

Time passed, and she emerged from the sea and after drying herself and dressing, she climbed onto the rocks and kissed each flower, scattering them over the water.

She felt Robbie was finally at peace and this little cove would be their special place where she could come and spend time with him. Walking back up the path to the villa, she felt calm.

Unbeknown to Sam, she and Robbie had not been alone. A dark figure hiding in the bushes at the top of the cliff had been watching her every movement.

He had been standing there for some time and as soon as he heard footsteps approaching he followed, taking care not to be seen. It didn't occur to him that this was a private moment. He just stared fixated with the scene in front of him. He'd never experienced such emotion as he watched this young woman expressing so much love in this last act of saying goodbye to somebody who meant everything to her. He collapsed to his knees and wept in utter despair for himself and his own misery.

*

It was turning into a hot summer. Already the temperature in the early hours was quite humid. Martha was struggling to acclimatise to the change, and she soon slipped into a routine of waking early, unable to go back to sleep. Stepping out of bed and heading towards the balcony and her comfy chair she wrapped a large soft shawl around her body as she sat and watched the sunrise. For the last couple of weeks, she had noticed John was out and about, too. Sometimes in the night, the sounds of someone in distress had woken her. At first, she thought it was a wild animal in the distance, but now she was sure it was John. It disturbed her to imagine he was suffering. He had told her about his active service in the army but seemed reluctant to talk about it, quickly changing the subject. If only she could find the right opportunity to help him. During the day he seemed OK, but sometimes, as it went dark, she saw him glancing around as though making sure there was nobody behind him. He was an enigmatic character, but she trusted her instincts about him and enjoyed his company.

Maybe he was suffering from post-traumatic stress? Several times, just before dawn, she had seen a dark shadow in the trees. Poor John. She didn't know what he was doing wandering around outside. Obviously, he found sleeping a problem like it was for her. There he was again, coming out from the vineyard. His dark figure was silhouetted by the early dawn light. Martha screwed her eyes to focus. He was carrying something in his arms. As he got closer, she realised it was a dog. He stood below Martha's balcony and shouted to her.

"Look at this little chap. I found him cowering behind the shrubbery. He looks lost."

"Oh, the poor thing. Bring him in John and give him some water. I'll meet you in the kitchen."

Together they looked at the poor creature.

"He doesn't appear to be hurt," John said. "I've checked him over. What would you like to eat, little chap?"

Martha came over with a bowl of water. "Try him with this John, he must be thirsty. I'll get him some milk and bread. Let's see how he takes to that. What breed do you think he is?"

"Judging by his long ears, he's got some spaniel in him."

"What are we going to do with him? Do you want to keep him?"

"I would love to. He looks like a stray. I'll take him to the vet later and get him checked out. Is there one locally?"

"There is good surgery in Piano Di Sorrento. I'll give them a ring and say you are calling in. We could put some posters up around the villa to see if anyone claims him. If nobody comes forward, he can stay with us. It would be nice to have a dog around the place."

"He certainly needs looking after. What shall we call him?"

Martha looked at the scruffy dog.

"When I was a child, I named my dog, Alfonso. I loved him dearly and was inconsolable when he died. I said I would never have another one. It's too painful when they leave you."

"Life's painful, Martha. If we love deeply we get hurt when something happens, but if we cover our emotions up, then we are protecting ourselves but not really feeling alive."

"Do you believe that happened to you, John? You

121

know, with all the things you must have gone through in the army?"

John surprised by the sudden question didn't answer for a moment and then said.

"Yes, that is what's wrong with me. I've been in a vacuum, getting angry for no reason, not sleeping. I just felt lonely. It's my fault. I've only realised this when I came here. I'm enjoying this new life and talking to people again. In fact, I'm just loving the beauty and colour it's making me appreciate that the world can be a wonderful place."

"That is nice to hear John, I'm so pleased. I've been a little worried about you, but I won't worry anymore. Oh look, he's taken to you. You have a friend for life."

The dog was resting his head on John's foot, having devoured his food.

"There, there, little fella, you are safe now," he said as he stroked the dog's face.

A soft expression had come over John. He'd always loved animals, especially when he joined the army and asked to go in the Horse Guards. It was his pride and joy to groom and make sure his horse was well. The smell of the stables and animals was where he belonged. Maybe a little dog to love was just what he needed, and he could make this little chap's life happy.

"Alfie would be a good name for him. Do you agree, Martha?"

"I do, it's perfect."

"Come on, Alfie, I'll take you to my room for a little sleep. Thanks, Martha for the chat."

"Anytime John, I'm always here."

*

It was getting towards the end of the evening. Everyone was winding down, and a peaceful atmosphere filled the air. Romantic songs on the music system encouraged a young couple to take to the floor and dance.

No one saw the figure emerge from the shadows of the orange trees. He seated himself at an empty table, and Mary just glimpsed him out of the corner of her eye.

Menus in hand, she approached him. "Good Evening Sir, I'm afraid the evening menu has finished, but I can offer you freshly made pizza or maybe pasta?"

He stared at her directly, and then his eyes wandered down to her neck and stared hard. Mary assumed he was looking at her chest. She immediately felt a chill. There was something about him that disturbed her. He did not respond to her welcoming smile. Eventually, he spoke abruptly in Italian.

"Pizza Margarita, senza condimenti e una birra." (Margarita pizza, no toppings, and a beer.)

"Si, subito." She smiled and walked back to the kitchen.

"Sorry, Eva, one more order, but it's for a plain Margarita for one."

"Oh, OK there is still time the pizza oven is going strong."

She headed for the fridge, shouting as she went "Anyone for a slice of pizza while I'm making one?"

"Si, Si, they all shouted back."

Mary turned to John.

"That guy over there. He's strange. He kept staring at my chest!"

"We are in Italy, Mary. I would have thought you'd got used to that."

She laughed. "I don't think I'll ever get used to it, but this guy is different. He's quite creepy."

"Where is he?" John asked, and Martha pointed to the table on the edge of the terrace.

"Over there, sitting on his own. He's dressed all in black."

John followed her gaze. "I can't see anyone."

"Well, really!" Mary exclaimed. "Eva, he's gone. Forget the pizza.

*

FRANCESCO

Eva stepped into the kitchen, stopping for a moment to gaze around. It looked so different from the first time she saw it. Now it was a vibrant place, full of noise and laughter. The smell of freshly baked bread penetrated the room.

Signor Miccio was singing a Neapolitan love song. He was sitting at a table painting a flower design onto the front of the day's menus. He loved this kitchen and was always here on his day off. Eva often asked for his advice, and he was more than happy to pass on his knowledge and expertise.

"Eva," her sous chef shouted. "A fisherman is here with today's catch. He is hoping we will place an order with him."

She headed for the patio garden. A smart man, in his early forties, stood waiting. A large navy blue apron was tied around his waist and his grey hair and beard were expertly groomed. He greeted her with a smile. His hand reached out to hers as he introduced himself.

"Buongiorno, Signorina. My name is Francesco Pascali. I came myself as I heard such excellent reports about your restaurant. It is the talk of the town. I was hoping you might be interested in our fresh fish products?"

He looked at the young girl in front of him, waiting for a response, but there wasn't any. Eva was frozen to the spot.

"As a gesture of goodwill, I hope today you will choose some fish with my compliments. We supply most of the top hotels and restaurants in this area. I have some magnificent octopus, shellfish, swordfish, tuna, clams, whatever you need."

"Did you say your name was Francesco Pascale? Do you live in Marina Grande?" her voice trembled as she spoke.

"Yes, Signorina, that is correct. My family have lived there for many years. I own the beach and waterfront. You are welcome to call at any time. I am often near the boatyard. I am rebuilding an old lugger boat, it is my passion!"

"Thank you, Signor Pascale. I'm afraid I have to go, but I will send my sous chef to choose some fish. I'm sure we'll meet again."

She rushed back towards the kitchen and shouted to

Henrik.

"Can you choose some fish from Signor Pascale for me, please?" She rushed upstairs to her room. Rummaging in her bag, she pulled out the photograph of her father. Yes, It is the same person even with a beard and grey hair. It is definitely him.

Her body seemed out of control as she sat on the edge of her bed, shaking from head to foot.

"It is him," her brain screamed at her ... my father!

A knock at the door brought her back to reality. John shouted through the door.

"Eva, are you OK? I watched you run through the kitchen. Can I help?"

She opened the door.

He put his arms around her as deep sobs rippled through her body.

"What on earth is the matter? It can't be that bad?"

"I've seen him," she cried.

"Who? Is someone bothering you? If so, I will soon sort them out."

"No, John, it is nothing like that. The fisherman outside he ... he is my father. I recognised him from this old photograph. I came to Sorrento to search for him.

"Are you sure, Eva? This is too serious to make a mistake."

"I'm positive. He introduced himself; it's the same name. Look at the photograph."

"Where is he now?"

"He's talking to Henrik in the garden about ordering our fish supplies through him."

"Stay here I'll check him out. Can I borrow this?"

She thrust the photograph into his hands.

"Yes, please. Come back and tell me what you think."

He made his way to the outside courtyard. Francesco was still there, showing off his array of fish, which was beautifully displayed with lemons, limes, and crushed ice.

"Buongiorno, Signor. My name is John Evans and I'm the Manager."

"Come and see, John. Signor Pascale has some beautiful fish. We should place an order. We need a good supplier and the quality is really excellent."

John offered his hand to Francesco. Immediately he recognised him from the photograph.

"I'm sure we can come to some arrangement, Signor," he said, quickly glancing at the fish. "If you leave your details with Henrik, we will certainly be in touch. Excuse me, I must dash." They shook hands, and John walked away, heading for Eva's room.

He knocked at the door. "Eva, it's me. Can I come in?"

She opened the door and without hesitation said. "It is him, isn't it?"

"Yes, I'm positive," John, replied. "What are you going to do?"

"I have no idea. He doesn't know about me. My mother died, and I found a letter and a photograph." She stuttered over her words. "She had a holiday romance and…"

"Sit down, Eva. So you came here to find your father?"

"Yes, I did. I needed to know who he is and whether he was still alive, and if so, does he want me in his life? It was such a shock this morning. I didn't expect it to be like this. I hoped I would just find him and then figure out how to approach him." She leaned forward. "John, what should I do?"

"You need to tell him, but just find the right moment.

131

Maybe get to know him and see if you like him? Visit his business? Perhaps Mary will go with you?"

"I'll ask her. I'm sure she will."

"If not, I'm always here." He smiled.

"Thank you, John. I feel so much better now. I should get back to the kitchen."

It was later that evening when Eva had a chance to talk to Mary. She was sitting outside in the cool air, taking a break from the kitchen after another hectic evening. She had tried to put to one side all thoughts of her father, but now, sitting by the lemon trees, she allowed herself to reflect on the meeting that morning.

"Hi Eva, I've brought you a glass of wine and some food. I'm famished." Mary said as she sat down next to her and tucked into a plate of gnocchi. "Wow, I need to take my shoes off! It's been pretty full, on, hasn't it? It was great watching Martha enjoying the company of her friend? I've never heard her laugh so loudly. She looked twenty years younger."

Eva interrupted. "I've got some news."

Mary reached for her glass. She could see Eva was excited about something.

"I've found my father,"

"When… where?" she spluttered as she tried to take in this news.

He came to the restaurant this morning to sell fish. He owns part of the fishing rights and the beach. I knew it was him straight away from the photograph, and he introduced himself as Francesco Pascale.

"Are you absolutely sure? Does he look like his photo?"

"Yes, he does. I told John, and he checked him out and agrees. It is him, Mary."

"Gosh, I don't know what to say. It's wonderful news." She moved forward and touched the young woman's hand. "Any idea what you are going to do next?"

"Well, John suggested I visit his business. He said to call in anytime. I wondered if you might like to go with me? I would really value your opinion."

"Of course I will if that's what you want, but maybe you should go on your own." Eva was a little taken aback by Mary's comment, and then she continued to give her reasons. "I wouldn't want you to rely on me. It's far too personal and important."

"Perhaps you are right, Mary. I'm not thinking straight."

"If it was me, I would go in there and tell him straight. It is going to be difficult, but he is either going to be thrilled or he's going to run for the hills."

"But what if he is married? He may have kids?"

"Eva, you must put yourself first. You've been without your father all your life, and your mum wasn't honest with you. If he's not happy about the situation, you will just have to accept this and carry on with your life. It will be his loss. Surely he wouldn't be that cruel? You are such a lovely girl. He will be very proud of you."

"Oh, Mary, you are so different from me. I wish I was more like you and be able to deal with this kind of thing."

"You are very young. I've spent my life having to do everything myself. What I have learned is if I want to be happy, I need to take control and make my own decisions. I've made some terrible ones but, in your situation, my gut feeling is that he has a right to be told you are his daughter. The next step is for him to work out for himself how he is going to deal with the news when you tell him about your mum. If he is worthy of being a father to you, then he will react in the right way." Mary reached over and touched Eva's hand. "Give it a couple of days to reflect, perhaps discuss it with Martha. She is wise and may have a different opinion from me. But, don't worry, it's amazing news and the way it has happened it's quite incredible it's a bit like life is pointing you in the right direction."

They sat, each in their own thoughts. Mary watched as Henrik drove off on his Vespa, heading for home.

"Here's a plan, Eva. Why not ask Henrik to go with you? He is your sous chef after all, and he can give you an unbiased opinion, as he doesn't know about your dad. He's a sensible guy. Invite Francesco and his family for a meal here, and then you will find out his circumstances. I agree, if he is married it could complicate the issue for you."

"I like that idea, sort of treat it like a business meeting and then when I'm sure I can take the next step."

A couple of hours later, Mary was lying in bed, trying to sleep. She felt a stab of guilt. Had she been hard on Eva, saying she didn't want to go with her? But there was no way she could go. He would recognise her. '*How on earth am I going to deal with this problem?*' she questioned herself. There was nobody she could talk to. The only thing she could do was to wait and see what happens and, in the meantime, avoid Franco like the plague.

*

Marina Grande, the tiny fishing village in Sorrento, was getting busy with tourists who wandered around taking photographs of the traditional houses. Local people loved its old rustic charm set against the lapping turquoise sea. Young children splashed in the water while their mothers chatted and sunbathed on the gritty sand. Henrik parked his Vespa by the waterfront.

"I think the warehouse is over there?" Eva said, pointing to a large building. "Oh, look, there he is."

Henrik led the way and Eva, unsure how this meeting was going to go, let him take the lead.

"Buongiorno, Signor," Henrik offered his hand. "We met at the villa the other day. My name is Henrik. I am Eva's sous chef."

Franco shook the young man's hand and turned to Eva.

"Buongiorno signorina, benvenuta." Speaking in English, he said warmly. "I am so happy you took my invitation to visit my empire."

Eva smiled. "Buongiorno, Signor, we have been looking forward to the visit."

"Come, follow me. I'll show you around." Franco led them into the cool warehouse. "My fishermen are out all night. They return around four in the morning to unload, clean, and gut the fish to prepare for orders. We keep everything clean and chilled. As you can see, we have already delivered today's catch to our customers."

Henrik looked around. The cleanliness of the warehouse impressed him.

"Signor Pascale," Eva said. "I will be happy to place our fish orders through you. We have been delighted with the freshness and quality you provide."

"Grazie, Signorina. May I offer you some refreshments? Perhaps a coffee or something cool?"

"Yes, we would like that."

They sat outside in the shade of a cafe.

"I understand the restaurant is very successful?" Franco said as he smiled at the two young people.

"It has gone better than we could have imagined, hasn't it, Henrik?"

"Yes, we are already seeing local people return, so that is an excellent result."

"Perhaps, Signor…"

"Please, Signorina, call me Franco. It makes me feel younger."

"Franco, perhaps you and your wife would care to join us on Saturday evening as our guests? We are having a 'British night' with a variety of our traditional foods. There will be lots of English desserts or puddings, as we call them, and music and dancing. You would be very welcome."

"That is most kind. Sadly, my wife and baby died a few years ago. I am on my own, but I would be honoured."

Eva had gone quiet. A voice in her head was screaming, "Tell him now." She turned to Henrik. "I think we should get back. We have a busy day ahead. I just want a private word with Franco. Can I meet you in a few minutes?"

"Of course, boss. I'll be by my Vespa. See you there."

He shook Franco's hand and said, "I'll phone in our order when I return."

"Thank you, that is so kind. Now Signorina, how can I help you?"

Eva had decided this was the moment to tell him. She reached into her bag and pulled out her mother's letter.

"I came to Sorrento with a purpose. I am looking for my biological father. My mother was here twenty two years ago, and she had a holiday romance." She clutched the photograph. "This is difficult for me to say but... but." She hesitated and then showed him the picture her mother had taken all those years ago.

"Mamma Mia. This photograph is of me? I don't understand?"

"I am the result of their romance," Eva spoke calmly, suddenly feeling in control now she had told him. "This is a letter my mother wrote to you, but she didn't send it. I only found it a year ago after she had died. Then when you came to the villa, the other day, I recognised you." Franco's hands were shaking. "I'm your *father*?" Disbelief was creeping into his voice.

"Yes. I think so. I appreciate you must be in shock. I

will go now and give you time to think. If you would like to meet again, I would be thrilled. Yes, I'll leave you in peace. You know where to find me."

She got up and headed for Henrik. They drove off and Eva didn't glance back. If she had, she would have seen Franco sitting, reading the letter and looking very puzzled.

Three days after Eva had broken the news to Franco that she was his daughter, a courier arrived with a small package. The kitchen was busy preparing for the day ahead, and John took delivery of it.

"Eva, this is for you." He said as he passed it to her. She ripped it open to find a small jewellery box containing a neat amethyst and gold bracelet with an accompanying note.

'I hope, Eva, you will accept this small gift and also agree to meet me tomorrow for lunch at Eduardo's Ristorante. I would like to talk and get to know you. The restaurant is on the waterfront in Marina Grande. Would 12.30 pm be suitable for you? Of course, if tomorrow is difficult, telephone me so we can make another time. If not, I look forward to seeing you.'

Samantha squealed with delight. "Oh, Eva, what an exquisite bracelet."

Mary inspected it. A thought went through her mind, '*Franco always had great taste in jewellery.*' She smiled at Eva.

"I'm so happy you have found your father."

"Thank you. I can't quite believe it. He wants to meet me for lunch tomorrow. I'm so excited. I must show this to Martha."

"I'll come with you," Sam said, grabbing Eva's arm. "I can't wait to see her face. Are you coming, Mary?"

John looked at Mary. She had gone quiet. He could tell by her face that something was bothering her, but had no idea what.

"Such good news, Mary, don't you think?"

"Yes, John, it is wonderful," Mary, replied as she walked out of the room.

*

Franco stared at his reflection in the mirror. His dark brown eyes revealed to the world his feelings, but now they appeared dull and expressionless. He'd tossed and turned most of the night and finally gave up on sleep instead wandered aimlessly around his house. He stared from his window. Dawn was breaking over the Bay of Naples, sending golden shimmers of light onto the tranquil Mediterranean Sea, and promising a beautiful day ahead.

I have a daughter,' he cried. Every time he repeated these words to himself, it wouldn't sink in. His mind kept drifting back over the years. He had no recollection of Eva's mother. Was he so selfish just living for pretty foreign girls who came on holiday and were looking for romance with Italian boys? Impressionable young women seduced by warm sunny evenings, a boy with laughing eyes, whispering beautiful words. So unlike the grey dreary lives, they lived at home. No wonder his charms were irresistible. Now he realised the sadness and emotional upset that resulted from a few moments of passion. Of course, he loved the girls he met. They were all beautiful to him. He also enjoyed being seduced by romance, and why not? How wonderful to see the adoring look in their eyes. He had felt like the most desirable man alive.

After their holiday ended and it was time for them to go home, his eyes would fill with tears as a girlfriend got on the coach to the airport. His sadness didn't last long. Another bus would arrive filled with pretty girls, some blonde, and some brunette. All with smiling faces, eager to get to know him until the day when Mary stepped into his life. There was something different about her, challenging and exciting. It wasn't long before the tables were turned and he found himself hopelessly in love.

He looked again at his reflection. Mary was always in his thoughts. He often wondered if he would ever see her again? Although in his mid-forties he was still a handsome man, and the stress of a loveless marriage to his Italian girlfriend and her subsequent death had taken a toll on him. He struggled to recover. His guilt, which haunted his nights, was even harder to bear. Why couldn't he have loved his wife? She was a traditional Italian woman deserving love and to be loved by her husband and children and have a good man to provide for her. The longed-for news that she was pregnant lifted both their spirits. For a time, life became happier. It gave them hope for something that would bring them closer together.

But it wasn't to be. Caterina and their baby, Madelena, died during a traumatic birth. The only peace he could find was from his business and his boat. He put all his energy and thoughts into turning his fishing enterprise into a successful living. It was his way of surviving and have some kind of normal life.

His thoughts came back to Eva. He rushed to change. How on earth could he make it up to her after she had lost her mother? But how could she like him when he wasn't sure he liked himself?

He closed the old oak door to his building and stepped out into the bright sunshine. He knew, without doubt, that he wanted to be a father to her, and now it was time to make this happen.

*

Eva was discussing with Martha and Samantha what to wear for her lunch with Franco. Martha sensed the nervousness in her and gave her some invaluable advice.

"Listen, my darling girl, try not to worry about today. Remember, the ball is in your court, so to speak. I'm sure your father is as nervous as you are, but don't forget you are in control. Keep your composure, don't talk too much, let him do that, and relax and see how you feel about him. You do not need to impress him, he's not your new boyfriend or boss but he is your father and, I am sure, will want to make it up to you."

"But what if he doesn't like me?" Eva whispered her fears as she picked up a blue skirt but rejected it and tossed it on the bed.

"Eva, how could he not like you? You are beautiful in every way. You have a kind nature, yet a strength and determination to succeed in everything you do. My dear girl, you don't even need to consider that possibility. He will be so proud of you. Believe me, I understand men." She smiled as Eva grasped her hand.

"Oh Martha, thank you. You are right. I'm going to meet my dad with my head high and if he can't see who I am, well, it's his problem."

"Good girl, now what are you going to wear?"

Samantha turned to both women.

145

"This," and she held up a pale coffee-coloured cotton dress with a halter neck. "It will complement your sun-tan and oh, these orange sandals... you will look fabulous."

*

Franco arrived early at the restaurant. He didn't want to be late.

"Ciao, Franco. Come stai e bello andare a vederti."

"Ciao, Eduardo. I'm well and it is good to see you too. It's been a long time."

"It has." Eduardo gave his friend a big hug. "Are you here to eat or to sell me some more fish?" He laughed and with a twinkle in his eye said; "You know that I've been a customer for years."

Franco grinned. "My best customer, my friend. Now I need a quiet table for two and, if possible, overlooking the sea."

"Mamma Mia, a romantic table for two. Is this for a new girlfriend? It's time you got back into seeing women again, it's been far too long."

Sorry to disappoint you, but I'm meeting my daughter -

my English daughter."

Eduardo's face lit up with this news.

"Your daughter?"

He was just about to answer when Eva came into the restaurant. For a second Franco stared. She looked stunning, a big welcoming smile on her face and her arms outstretched in greeting.

Eduardo stepped back and watched as Franco moved forward to welcome her.

"Ciao Eva, Beneventa e cosi bello vederti,"

"Ciao Franco, it's lovely to see you too." They hugged, clinging to each other for a moment.

Franco, turning to Eduardo, said. "Let me introduce you to my daughter, Eva."

Eduardo moved forward to shake hands, but Eva went straight for a welcoming hug.

"It is such a pleasure to meet you Eduardo and what a beautiful restaurant you have."

"Grazia, Signorina, let me show you to your table. Is this one to your liking it is close to the water and has a beautiful view?"

"E perfetto, grazie mille," she said.

"Tu parli Italiano," he asked.

"No, but I'm learning." She smiled at both men.

Franco started to relax. He found her friendliness genuine and charming. The similarity in her eyes to his was clear to see. Her quick natural smile was so infectious he couldn't help but grin like a child.

Eva leaned forward, touching Franco's hand. "It's beautiful here. Listen to the sound of the sea lapping against the jetty. It's perfect."

"It is," he replied. "My father used to own this building. It was part of his fishing business. After he died, it passed to my brother and me. Then we sold it to Eduardo, as we needed money. He's made it interesting by extending the restaurant over the sea."

"Oh, Franco, look at that," Eva pointed to a turtle swimming below them in the shallow green water.

"Ah, that is Nello. He has been here for years. Every day he comes and the staff throws him fish scraps and bits of vegetables. Eduardo is waiting for someone to ask for turtle soup."

Eva looked horrified.

"Don't worry," Franco laughed. "Nobody ever has and

and I do not think Eduardo would even think of putting Nello in a pot, he's too fond of him."

Eduardo appeared at their table, and with a flourish produced his menu.

"Signorina, we have, for our specialty of the day, a delicious platter of mixed seafood, octopus, prawns, oysters or, if you prefer, I can recommend chef's home made fresh pasta with various sauces."

They agreed on a seafood platter, and Eduardo headed back to the kitchen.

Franco poured Eva a large glass of Librandi Critone. "I think you will enjoy this wine. It is from Calabria and a perfect choice for our lunch."

"Thank you," Eva sipped slowly. "I do like it. Do you know a lot about wines?"

"Of course, but only Italian ones."

"I may need your advice for my menus in the restaurant."

"Oh, I'm sure I can point you in the right direction."

Eva smiled. The conversation was going well, and Franco appeared relaxed.

"You mentioned your brother? Does he work with you

in your business?"

"No, no, Luca has been living in the States for a few years and persuaded me to go over and invest in his restaurant in Chicago."

"Did you go?"

"I did, I stayed for five years."

"Why did you come back home?"

Franco motioned to Eduardo for a bottle of aqua minerale and, his face showing a flicker of emotion replied. "I was unhappy and missed my life here. In my heart, I am a fisherman and love the sea and warmth. Chicago was, well what can I say, suffocating me… and so cold." He hesitated for a moment and said. "To be honest, when my brother suggested I join him, I jumped at the chance. My wife and child had died. I was in a dark place."

"Oh, I'm so sorry. I can't imagine how hard that must have been for you?"

"It was difficult to talk about. On the bright side, I learned English, which I am so grateful for now."

"Perhaps you needed a chance for a different life? I can understand that. It's been hard at times for me too, losing my stepfather when I was 14 and my mother struggled with life, and then she died."

"How did she die, Eva?" he asked.

"She took to alcohol and anti-depressants and it all got out of hand until one day she overdosed and I found her when I came home from school. The medics couldn't revive her and well, that was that."

"Mia cara ragazza. Mi dispiace molto." (My dear girl. I'm so sorry)

His voice was emotional but Eva knew what he meant. She smiled. "I've moved on now and I've found you and I hope, with time, we can get to know each other?"

"For me, it would give me great pleasure. I cannot find the words to express how wonderful it is that you wanted to find me and make contact although it is very sad for your mother. I also regret that I was not in your life. I'm sorry to have let you down."

"How have you let me down if you didn't know about me? We cannot change what has happened, but we can move forward."

She smiled and touched his hand. "I love it here in Sorrento. It is beautiful and the chance Martha has given me to prove myself is just amazing, I am so happy right now, especially as I have found you and whatever happens, it is up to both of us to work things out. We may have different backgrounds, but I'm hoping our blood tie will bring us close together."

Franco stared at his daughter. For him, this was a moment he could only have dreamed of. For a long time, his life had been empty and without direction. Now he had a daughter. Someone to love and to love him, and he would not let this slip away. Eva sensed her father was getting emotional.

"Come on, I'm going to let you buy me my first gelato." She said.

Tears filled his eyes, and quickly he recovered his composure.

"Eva, mio cara, I am going to buy you the biggest ice cream you have ever seen."

They stepped away from the table and headed out into the brilliant sunshine, their arms linked together.

*

It was late afternoon. Eva was walking back from Sorrento after doing some shopping. She was never sure what to do on her day off. Her life was so busy. It was relaxing to get away from the villa for a few hours and enjoy her surroundings. Everything was going well. The restaurant was going from strength to strength, and now she had her father in her life. She had never been this happy.

Trudging up the long hill to the villa, she heard someone call her name. "Eva," She turned around and was delighted to see Henrik sliding to a halt next to her on his Vespa.

"Hi, what are you doing out here?" he said.

"I've been to Sorrento and now I'm on my way back to the villa."

"Do you need to go back? I'm going to St Agata to meet my friends. We are going to have some food and enjoy a game of boules. Come with me? You'll like them. It will do you good to have some fun. You work far too hard."

Eva jumped at the chance to do something different.

"Yes, I'd love to."

She enjoyed being around Henrik he made her laugh. Now she had the chance to get to know this young Danish boy and to be included in a group of people her own age.

"Hold on tight. We are going up into the hills." He said as she got on the back of his Vespa and put her arms around his waist.

She felt exhilarated as he wound his way through the countryside. Glancing to her right, she caught glimpses of the sea. The scenery was changing as they moved around each bend.

"Here we are," Henrik yelled, and he pulled into a small clearing surrounded by shrubbery.

She could hear laughter and music close by.

"Come on, Eva, you'll enjoy this," and he put out his hand to help her up the steep slope.

It felt good to hold his hand, and she was happy for him to take the lead. His friends yelled out to him.

"Over here, Henrik."

She wasn't too sure what language it was, but she followed him and saw a group of young people, laughing as they played boules.

He introduced her to Hermann, from Munich, and his English girlfriend, Bridget. They both welcomed her with hugs.

"Hi Eva," Bridget greeted her. "Henrik has told us all about you. It's brilliant what you are doing at the villa."

"Thank you, that is so nice of you to say."

"We thought we would come over for a pizza one night."

"Oh, you must. It would be such fun."

Henrik interrupted. He'd gone to get some wine and bowls full of fresh bread, cheese, and grapes.

"Shall we sit on this bench? I don't know if you have played boules before? It's easy. All you have to do is throw the ball as near as you can to the jack, which is the small ball. You'll soon pick it up." He passed her some bread and cheese. "It's only simple, but to be honest, it is a refreshing change from the rich food we serve in the restaurant."

"It looks lovely." Eva glanced around her. "I love it here. It's very traditional and rustic." She looked towards the view and saw a small island very close to them.

"That's Capri," Henrik said as he dipped his crunchy

bread in a bowl of olive oil. "From here, you can't see the Bay of Naples anymore. We've come around the peninsular and are now nearer the Gulf of Salerno. If we had continued on the road, we would come to Positano and on to Amalfi. This area is mainly agriculture. Most of the farmers supply our fresh vegetables for the restaurant.

"I haven't had time to explore anywhere." Eva smiled. "There is so much to see. I had no idea how close Capri is. You can almost touch it."

Eva took a mouthful of fresh, crusty bread soaked in olive oil and tomatoes. "Hmm… it tastes delicious." She took a sip of wine and pulled a face.

"It's very raw and cheap but goes well with the strong cheese. Here, try some." He smiled as he passed her the food. He was so glad she had agreed to come out with him. For a long time, he had hoped they might get together.

"Thanks for bringing me here. It's wonderful to be with people my age. I can't remember ever being part of a crowd."

Henrik had sensed that Eva was lonely. He desperately

wanted to get to know her better.

"Maybe this is what you need. You work too hard, Eva. Everyone needs to relax and have fun. If you like, I could teach you to ride a Vespa. It's easy."

She looked horrified. "Oh no! I've never learned to drive. I can't even ride a bicycle."

"Trust me, you'll soon get the hang of it."

"But what about the traffic? They drive like crazy."

"It's bluster. Just do what they are doing, but with more confidence. Nobody here follows the rules and Vespa's cannot go fast. It's fun. It will open up your life and you could come and join us. We all meet up at least once a week and ride somewhere where tourists don't go."

Eva smiled. She liked the idea of meeting new people.

"Who are your other friends, Henrik?"

"Well, the guy over there, hugging his girlfriend, is Claudio. He's Italian, and he is going out with Monica, who is English. She works in a hotel close by, and Claudio is a student studying Marine Biology in Naples. He's lucky he gets very long summer holidays. Hermann and Bridget, you've met. Hermann is a German teacher

157

in a school in Sorrento and Bridget; well she's a baker. She makes exceptional cakes and bread from her tiny bakery close to the beach at Massa Lubrense."

"Don't you have a girlfriend, Henrik?"

"I did, but she found Italian boys were..." he hesitated for a moment trying to find the right English word, "irresistible!" He smiled.

"I can't believe that she must be mad. You are such a lovely person."

"Thank you, that's a nice thing to say."

"I mean it, Henrik. I can't comment on Italian men. My father is from Italy. I've only just met him." She said.

"Sorry, I don't understand."

"Oh, it's a long story. You remember Franco from our meeting the other day?"

"The fisherman?"

"Yes, well, he is my father."

"I still don't understand!" Henrik said.

"Yes, it's true. I came to Italy to look for him. I only found out about him after my mother died." She looked embarrassed and wondered why she had brought the subject up. Eva continued. "He didn't know I existed."

"Really!"

"You remember when I said I needed a quick word with him and you waited for me? Well, I told him then that I was his daughter. He contacted me a couple of days later and he took me out for lunch." She leaned closer and whispered, "What did you think of him?" Realising she was putting him on the spot, she immediately said, "I'm sorry I shouldn't have asked you."

"Don't apologise. He's a nice guy. He was friendly and seemed genuine. His face looked quite sad, especially when he talked about losing his wife and baby. So how did he take the news?"

"Well, he was very shocked, but after he had time to take it all in it turned out better than I could have imagined."

He touched her hand. "I am so happy for you. It's quite an amazing story."

"Thank you." She didn't want to let go of his hand. "It's been good to speak about it. Anyway, I'm monopolising you. Shall we join your friends?"

"Monopolising? That's a new word for me."

"It means keeping you all to myself. Come on, let's

play bowls."

"Boules," he corrected her, and she smiled into his laughing face.

*

THE MONASTERY

(Il Monastero)

The centuries-old monastery towered over the hillside. The dark stonework construction gave the building a menacing appearance. Its tiny windows looked more like a prison than a place of prayer. Stone walls gave a coolness from the oppressive heat. The monks, who were elderly, lived a simple life. They produced their own food and spent a life of prayer and dedication to their religion. Brother Emmanuel was standing in front of his Abbot. He was worried and was glad to express his concerns.

"The young man, I'm worried about him, Father. He's gone missing again. It's been over two weeks since he disappeared."

"Yes, Brother. I have seen that he is returning to his old ways again. I hoped that working in the garden would bring him a little peace, and he appeared to be settling into our routine. Then this sudden change in his character is hard to cope with. I have feared for his safety, but also for the Brothers. I do not think it is fair to add this burden to their lives, as they are all quite frail. This young man is powerful. I will inform the police straight away. His behaviour has been causing me concern, and these dark moods are overwhelming and suffocating him."

The Abbot headed for his office. He closed the door and reached for the telephone. He didn't want to make this call, but knew the time had come. The police took down the details and promised to send an Inspector over to the monastery for more information. Later in the day, a police officer rang the giant doorbell, which clanged loudly all around the building. Brother Emmanuel welcomed him in and took him to see the Abbott.

"Thank you for coming." The Abbot motioned for him to sit. "Can I offer you some water? It is such a hot day."

"Thank you," the police officer said. He looked around the room, noting the starkness and lack of comfort.

"I understand you wish to report a missing person?"

"Yes, that is correct. About three months ago, we found a young man asleep in one of our greenhouses. He was thin and appeared troubled and homeless."

"Troubled?" queried the police officer.

"He was afraid of us and tried to move away when we went near him, like a wounded animal. We spoke to him calmly, but he wouldn't answer. In fact, the whole time he was with us, he didn't speak one word. We gave him food and a bed. After a time, he seemed less afraid. He stayed with us and settled into our routine well, spending his day tending to the vegetables and garden. He was quite helpful to our Brothers, who showed him a lot of kindness. They didn't ask him questions, and I believed he felt safe."

"Do you know where he had come from? What his name is?"

"No, he didn't speak. We prayed that one day he would open up to us so we could help him."

"And when did this young man go missing?"

Well, he would disappear for a day or two and just wander back here as though nothing had happened. We noticed he had cut marks on his arms and legs, we thought he had been self-harming. Sometimes he would have black moods and wouldn't come out of his room. Eventually, they would lift and he became more settled. Then two weeks ago he disappeared and has not returned. That is why I telephoned you. I am worried something has happened to him."

"I see. Is there anything else you can tell me about him? A description would be helpful. I can run a check on missing persons and maybe get a lead there."

"Well, let me think, 18 or 19 years old and quite tall, at least 6ft if not more, with black hair and brown eyes. When we spoke to him he understood what we were saying, but didn't reply. We assumed he is Italian, as he understood the Neapolitan dialect. The only clothes he had were the black jeans, and a ripped t-shirt he arrived in. Other than that, I can't add any more."

"We will see what we can do, and I'll report back to you. In the meantime, should he return, just let us know?"

"Thank you, officer. It is most kind of you. I'll show you the way out."

*

THE STALKER

Mary desperately needed to get away. The risk of bumping into Franco was real. She headed down to the sea. Reaching the vineyard, a van was coming up the long drive. Hiding behind the vines, she waited for it to pass her. A quick glance at the driver caused her heart to jump as she recognised Franco. Oh, how she longed to see him again and to put her arms around him. Tears filled her eyes. It was too much to bear.

'I have to go back to England; Eva has every right to get to know her father. If I keep making excuses not to meet her dad, she will get confused and wonder why.' Her thoughts crowded in her head.

She headed down the path towards the sea, hoping the cool air would somehow ease her thoughts. The heat of the sun became oppressive and didn't help her mood.

Reaching the beach and sitting on the rocks, she allowed the soft caress of the gentle waves to clear her head. Her thoughts drifted back to the time when she was so in love with Franco. Never in her life had she experienced such happiness as knowing, at last, there was someone in her life who loved her and she loved back. Being brought up in a children's home and never knowing her parents had left scars. But she survived through a determination to make a life for herself. Then she met Franco and everything changed. She experienced love, and she liked the excitement. It was seven months into their relationship when she became pregnant. An opportunity arose to tell him when he suggested a weekend away to celebrate her birthday. The setting was perfect. The restaurant was situated high in the mountains above Positano, in the tiny village of Montepertuso. As usual, he charmed and spoilt her until the moment came when she asked him about his family.

It didn't take long for her to realise that his life would go down the traditional route of marrying an Italian girl, and it hit her hard. The hurt became unbearable. How did she get it so wrong? Believing life would be the two of them and their child? Was it naïve of her to imagine he wanted this, too?

As soon as she could, she returned to London, not even explaining or saying goodbye. The indignity of having to turn to friends to put her up and the terrible ordeal of miscarrying was the ultimate rejection. The tears fell down her face.

"What on earth shall I do now?" she asked herself. Her life was a total mess. The thought of returning to her career as a flight attendant unsettled her. She needed someone to love, a purpose, something resembling normality, but she did not know how to move forward. The villa allowed her time to think about her future. She had bonded with the others, especially Eva, who was a spirited young woman, and her eagerness to succeed and make the restaurant something special was inspirational. Returning to Sorrento had made her realise she belonged here. Now it was all over.

Her mind just became tangled in thoughts. She breathed deeply, trying to calm herself. She had lost everything again, and it seemed her only option was to run away. But was it? Why should she have to leave the place that was her first proper home? It wasn't fair. Never had she felt so settled as she did now. Maybe if she told Eva about her relationship with Franco all those years ago, she would understand? Perhaps Franco had forgotten her? She could keep her distance and try to put the last twenty years behind her. Her decision was made, and she started walking back to the villa.

Stopping at the top of the path and glancing across to take in the view once more her mind felt more positive and at ease. Then hearing a loud cry, she turned around only to come face to face with a stranger rushing straight towards her, his face contorted with rage.

*

The evening service was just about to start. There was a gentle trickle of people heading up the driveway. Already they were enjoying the warm July evening and were taking in the beautiful views. The villa was in the most stunning location. Sorrento, with lights glittering in the distance, beckoned tourists to visit.

Eva sighed with contentment. Her kitchen was buzzing with laughter as the staff worked hard on the preparations for the evening. She loved the thrill and anticipation of preparing her dishes. As soon as service started, the adrenalin kicked in. Excitement took over, together with the anticipation that it was going to be a successful evening.

She was still on a high from her lunch with Franco a few days ago. It had gone better than she could have hoped for. Tonight he was coming to the restaurant to eat. She was hoping to impress him with her griddled swordfish and garlic, with a white wine sauce and mixed roasted baby vegetables.

Samantha popped her head around the French door.

"Eva, have you seen Mary? We are about to take orders, but I can't find her anywhere."

"No sorry, not since lunchtime. Giuseppe… quick I can smell burning–check the oven." She turned back to Sam. "Maybe John might know where she is. I'm sure there must be a reason. She's usually first in the restaurant."

"Don't worry, looks like you've enough on your plate. I'll ask him. If she turns up, tell her we need help. It looks like it's going to be a busy night again."

The evening sped by. There was no sign of Mary. Samantha, with the help of John, kept service to its usual high standard. The diners were enjoying themselves and Signor Miccio, who had popped in for a free meal, switched on a CD of the Three Tenors in concert. Suddenly, the restaurant became a crazy karaoke event encouraged by Signor Miccio. Diners were belting out renditions of 'Turno 'E Sorrento' and shouts of 'bravo' filled the air.

Martha was joining in with the laughter, and applause. Meanwhile, in the kitchen, everyone was busy and, although to the outside world it would appear chaotic, Eva had everything under control.

Franco had arrived to bring more supplies of fish, after receiving a panic phone call from Eva. He breezed into the kitchen, smiling and waving to everyone. John called him over.

"Ciao Franco."

"Ciao John, here is more fish for you."

"Let me take it off you. Oh, and Martha saw you arrive, and she wonders if you are free to join her for dinner. She is quite eager to meet you. Eva has told her all about you."

"It would delight me greatly."

Eva overheard the conversation and straight away said "She is excited to get to know you."

"Follow me," John replied as he led him to the terrace.

Martha stood up and warmly shook Franco's hand. "It is such a pleasure to meet you at last. I'm so pleased you are joining me for dinner."

"The pleasure is all mine, Signora, and I must congratulate you on your beautiful villa and restaurant."

Martha smiled. "I couldn't have done it without these amazing young people coming into my life and giving me a whole new direction. I think it was Eva, with her enthusiasm for the old kitchen and her vision of how it could be. It was the inspiration I needed."

John handed out the menus, and it wasn't long before Samantha arrived with their food.

"You must try this starter, Franco. It's salmon and watercress mouse. It just melts in the mouth." Martha said as she poured him a glass of wine.

They settled into their courses, chattering away in Italian, which for Martha was always a delight. Franco spoke of his memories of growing up in Sorrento and about his parents. It fascinated Martha, she was always keen to hear what had happened to the locals and Franco was impressed when she remembered certain characters, in particular Guido, who had a horse and carriage in Piazza Tasso. Everyone knew him. His grumpy attitude towards life was always a cause of laughter. Franco described everyone's reactions when he died.

"The entire town came out and lined the streets for his funeral. It was so silent as the hearse came up the road. But what made everyone cry was Hercules, his horse. He had a giant black feather on his head and it almost touched the floor when he drooped his head as he slowly walked in front of the coffin. It was very moving. Afterward, there was a big party and later we discovered

Guido had left his entire estate to Hercules so he would be taken care of for the rest of his life. Everyone knew Guido loved his horse even though he grumbled about how lazy and useless he was."

"I would love to have seen that," Martha chuckled. "I do remember him."

Eva appeared, carrying a small Tia Maria for Martha and a coffee for her father.

"How was everything?" she inquired tentatively.

"The swordfish was delicious and the flavour," Franco put his fingers to his lips. "Your recipes are quite different, cara, and exciting."

"It was wonderful, Eva, as always. It would equal any top-class restaurant in London. Are you joining us, dear? Your father and I are having such a lovely time, I'm really enjoying myself."

"I wish I could, Martha, but I must get back. Customers are waiting for desserts and I promised Signor Miccio a special pizza. He popped over on his day off from the hotel just to see how things were going. He's spent the entire evening going from table to table flirting with the ladies and encouraging everyone to join in with

175

his singing."

"Yes, we heard him. He is an asset to the hotel. I've been trying to persuade him to come here and work for us, but the hotel is his passion so we'll just be grateful he comes in his free time. Where is John, by the way? And Mary? I haven't seen her this evening."

"Oh Martha, Mary hasn't been here since this morning. We can't understand what has happened to her. You don't know where she might be, do you?"

"No, my dear. How strange, it's not like Mary to disappear without telling anyone. She's normally so thoughtful."

"Well, John is very worried. He's gone looking for her. To be honest, she was acting strange this morning. I hope she hasn't had bad news from home or anything."

"I suppose you have tried her phone?" Franco said.

"Yes, we rang her mobile but realised it was in her handbag which was hanging up in the kitchen."

"Try not to worry, Eva. I'm sure there is a reasonable explanation. Please let me know if John has any news."

"Of course I will, straight away. Well, if you two are OK, I'd better get back. I'll catch you both later."

"Eva, if John needs help, just tell me," Franco replied. He could see the concern on his daughter's face.

"Oh, I will." She shouted as she rushed back to the kitchen.

*

John headed off to search for Mary down at the small cove. In his mind, he was trying to eliminate potential hazards, but knew that it was getting late and that darkness would soon make it difficult to look for her. The sea could be a source of danger. Even though the Mediterranean was calm, jagged rocks were hard to see. If Mary had gone for a swim to cool down in the heat, she may have got into difficulties. He was hoping there was another reason for her disappearance.

Soon he was staring at the clear turquoise sea as it gently lapped against the rocks. He searched the small beach for any signs. The old boathouse still looked undisturbed, with no signs of Mary's towels or clothing, just some old rags and rubbish.

He headed back up the steep winding path towards the villa, carefully looking on either side to make sure he had missed nothing. His army training had taught him to spot signs of broken foliage or disturbance. Alfie was barking and had stopped at the top of the hill. Then John spotted her lying twisted on a small ledge. He scrambled down, holding on to branches and bracken and making sure not to fall himself.

"Oh, my God, Mary." She was unconscious. He could see from her skin colour that she was in a bad way. Without hesitating, he phoned the villa. Samantha answered.

"Sam, I've found her. She has fallen and is injured. Can you ring for an ambulance and air rescue if they have it? I'm about a quarter of a mile up from the boathouse on the left-hand side. She's lying about 12ft down the cliff on a small ledge. I think she may have banged her head. Her skin is bluish, and she is unconscious. Her heartbeat is slow, and so is her pulse. Please hurry and ring me back."

Samantha immediately shouted out to Franco. She explained the situation and asked him if he would speak to the medics. He made the call and then asked her to ring John to say help was on the way.

"I'm coming with you." Sam insisted as Franco headed off to join John. "Eva, can you pass me those clean towels and a bottle of water? Thanks."

She ran after Franco while speaking to John on his mobile. "How is she?"

"Not good. I'm not sure what to do to help."

"Just don't move her. We are almost there."

"OK, but please be quick."

A few minutes later, Franco scrambled down to him. Mary was lying crumpled on her side. He stared at her. "Maria," he whispered in disbelief.

"Let me through Franco please, I need to see her."

Franco moved back, as the ledge was so small.

Sam checked her pulse and covered her with the towels to keep her warm. Goodness knows how long she had been lying there.

"Is she going to be all right?" John said.

"I don't know. She's in shock and has a nasty head injury. I don't like her skin colour at all. I wish they would hurry."

In the distance, the sound of sirens filled the air. Franco headed back up to the villa. He was certain it was Mary, or Maria, as he affectionately called her. As soon as he saw her lying there, he had recognised her. He rushed to the ambulance and explained the urgency and the difficulty of where she had fallen. They followed him down the path and passed the medical bag to John as they climbed down.

The doctor assessed the situation and reached for his phone, sending for the air ambulance.

"John," Franco shouted. "I'm going back up to wait for the helicopter and make sure there is room to land. I'll bring them down."

The car park was almost free of cars. Most of the diners had gone, and the remaining customers hurried to move their vehicles out of the way.

Eva and Martha anxiously stood, clutching each other.

"Try not to worry and stand well back when the helicopter comes. It should be here any minute." Franco said.

It was five minutes later when they heard the roar of the engines. Franco stood in the centre of the car park and waved frantically. It must have been at least thirty minutes later when the doctors appeared, carrying Mary on a stretcher. They lifted her onto the aircraft and flew off toward Naples. Franco rushed to Eva, who had tears streaming down her face.

"Try not to worry, Eva. She's in expert hands."

Martha got up from her chair as John headed towards her.

"How is she?" Martha whispered, afraid of the answer.

John guided her back to her seat.

"It's not good," He said. "It looks like she has a fractured skull and a broken leg. They are worried because she hasn't regained consciousness. Will you both be all right? Franco has offered to drive me to the hospital in Naples."

"Yes, we will be fine. Please go, but ring as soon as you know anything."

"Of course we will."

Franco whispered to Eva, "take care of Martha. She is looking very frail."

"I will, I will."

The drive to Naples was long and the roads very busy, made worse by the emergence of a football crowd from Castellammare di Stabia. Franco kept his calm, but inside he was screaming.

"Do you think she will live?" Franco asked.

"I don't know."

"Maria, Maria," Franco cried out, his heart in pain.

Stunned by his cry, John looked at him.

"You mean Mary, don't you?"

"To me, she is Maria. I recognised her, John. I've spent the last twenty years with her face in my head."

"You are Mary's Franco? Oh my God, of course, it's all making sense now. She said she had come back to Italy looking for someone, but it never occurred to me it was you! She must have recognised you when you came to the villa. Oh, what a situation. You are Eva's father. How could she say anything to you – or Eva?"

"You said she came back for me?" Franco turned into a parking spot in the hospital forecourt and switched off the engine.

"Yes, she told me her reason to come here was to find you and get re-acquainted. You mean everything to her."

"Oh, no!" Tears sprang into his eyes.

"Let's see how she is. At least you have found each other again."

"But, John, it may be too late. I don't know what to do."

"Yes, you do. Come on, there is no time to waste."

*

Once the helicopter had set off, Samantha headed for Martha and Eva, who were waiting outside the restaurant door.

"How is the poor girl? Come and tell me what is happening?" Martha asked, her voice full of concern.

Samantha explained how John had found Mary and details about her injuries.

"Is she conscious?" Eva asked.

"No, and that is the worry."

"Oh dear, poor darling." Martha clutched the arms of her chair.

"Can I get you a drink, Martha, tea, or a brandy? It has been such a shock to us all, but we have to be positive. I'm sure she is in safe hands."

"Some warm milk would be lovely, Eva. I think I'll go to my room, but please let me know as soon as you hear anything. I doubt if I will sleep well tonight."

"I'll walk with you," Eva held Martha's arm. They walked together through the restaurant. Sam was in the kitchen when Eva returned.

"Do you want anything to eat, Sam? Are you hungry? You missed your break."

"No thanks, I can't face food at the moment."

"Do you think she will get through this all right?" Eva said.

"I don't know. I saw a lot of head injuries when I worked in A&E. We should prepare ourselves for the worst. It is serious. I'm praying she doesn't have any long-term problems if she comes through this."

"What happens now, Sam?"

"Well, I was wondering if she has any relatives we should contact, but I can't remember her mentioning anybody, can you?"

"No, she is such a private person. She said nothing about her life, except she used to live here about 20 years ago. That was why she came on holiday to renew some memories, but she didn't go into detail. She must have a family somewhere. We could contact British Airways. She worked for them for many years."

"That might be a good idea. Perhaps we should wait until we hear from John. We could ask one of the BA Reps they often come here for dinner. They get on so well with Mary, I'm sure they will try to get some information."

Eva's phone rang, and she rushed to answer it.

"Hi, it's John. We are going to stay at the hospital. They've taken Mary down to the theatre for treatment. Try not to worry and get some sleep. I'll ring you as soon as we get any news."

"Is Franco still with you?"

"Yes, he's been brilliant, translating everything, although there is not a lot of information at the moment. He's going to stay with me, which is great because I can't understand what they are saying."

"Tell him I'll talk to him tomorrow."

"OK, Eva, will do. I'll get off now."

"Bye, John, take care."

Martha stood in the doorway.

"Are you OK?" Sam asked as Martha moved into the kitchen and settled in a chair. "Can't you sleep?"

"There is something I must tell you, girls. I'm not easily frightened, but a few times, I've seen someone watching us. I often wake early to enjoy the dawn breaking, and sometimes I've spotted a man standing under the trees. I couldn't make him out, but now I realize he was staring at the villa. At first, I thought it was John, struggling to sleep or even sleepwalking. I don't know if you are aware, but he sometimes suffers from post-traumatic stress from his army days. I spoke to him about it when we first came to live here. He said sometimes he used to go for a walk through the vineyard. It was after he found Alfie it helped him to sleep better. Then, early this morning, I saw a movement in the trees. It was dark, and I assumed it was my imagination. But now I'm getting worried, especially about Mary's accident. I don't understand how she could have fallen?"

"You think someone attacked her?" said Sam.

"I'm not sure, Samantha. I needed to talk to you all about it. We are three women alone here."

Eva, without hesitating, said.

"We need to secure all the doors and windows and ring the police now."

Sam reached for her phone.

"Can you speak to them, Martha? I'm not sure my Italian is good enough."

"Yes, of course." Martha made the call.

*

It was a long night for John and Franco. They were in the waiting room and each time the door opened, they both jumped. But Mary was still in the operating theatre. Franco sat with his head in his hands. He couldn't understand what was happening. Had Mary really come back to find him? And to discover he had a daughter who was also looking for him, it was all so incredible. He sighed. All those wasted years and now this … it was too much to take in.

"John, does Eva know Mary was looking for me?"

"I don't think she does. Mary gave little away about herself. She is such a cheerful person, getting on with everything with enthusiasm and being there for everyone else." John thought for a moment. 'I think we need to contact Mary's family, but I can't remember her speaking about them. Did she mention anything to you?"

"No, John, it's been over twenty years since Mary and I were together. I remember she told me a little about her childhood. It wasn't good. She was brought up in care. Had a few foster homes, but she didn't want to talk about it. As you say, she was happy and wanted to live in the present. I don't know how I am going to explain to Eva about Mary and what she means to me." Franco stood up and walked around the room, wringing his hands in agitation. "Oh my God, John, I'm going to lose both of them."

"Now steady on. You are overthinking this. Eva is a very grounded young woman. What she needs is total honesty from you. When you explain the situation, she will understand. We must be positive and take one step at a time."

"Si, Si, you are right, grazie."

It was three hours later when a doctor appeared. He sat down next to them and spoke in Italian. John became concerned when the Doctor put his hand on Franco's shoulder to comfort him. He shook their hands and left them alone.

"What did he say?" John said.

"Mary has come through the operation. She had a bleed on her brain because of a severe head injury. The next 24 hours are crucial. They have put her under heavy sedation. It could go either way. Also, her leg is broken."

"Can we see her?" John asked.

"No, only next of kin can go into the intensive care unit.

The doctor suggested we go home and come back or ring tomorrow. I think I'm going to stay, John, but you go. Here, take my keys."

"I will go back if you are sure you will be OK. It's 5 am so everyone will wake up soon. I guess they will be desperate for news. Don't worry; I'll get a taxi. Do you want me to mention anything to Eva?"

"No, I need to tell her myself. Just say, I'm staying here, because of the language problem and I'll be in touch soon."

"OK, take care, mate. Ring if you have any news."

John hailed a taxi. It wasn't long before he was heading back to the villa. The dawn was breaking, bringing in a new day, but he was too tired to care. He couldn't quite get to grips with the way Mary had fallen. It had been perfect weather and the path, although steep and rough, was wide enough not to go too close to the edge. A thought had been niggling in his mind for some time. Whenever he sensed he was being watched, he'd persuaded himself it was all in his mind. But what if someone really was out there watching them?

*

The journey back seemed endless; he was getting increasingly anxious about everybody back home.

Upon reaching the villa, he was surprised to see it all shut up, with no signs of movement. He approached the door, only to find it locked. Reaching for his key, he was greeted by an excited Alfie who was barking loudly, delighted to see him.

"Hello young man," John said. "Where is everybody?"

Samantha appeared at the top of the stairs.

"It's John," she shouted.

"Morning, what's going on? Are you all OK?"

"Yes, John, we are fine. Come into the kitchen and up date us on Mary. Do you want some breakfast?"

"Yes, please, Sam. I'm sorry to say Mary is not too good. They've managed to stop a bleed on her brain and her leg is badly broken. She is under heavy sedation. Franco insisted on staying at the hospital and will phone if anything changes."

"How kind of him," Eva said, pleased that someone was with Mary.

"I offered to stay, but as Franco pointed out, my Italian is basic and medical terms are hard to understand, even if you are fluent. He was quite comfortable and said he would speak to you soon. How are things here?" John asked. "Are you coping OK?"

Samantha looked at Martha.

"We are not sure, John. Martha has seen a stranger, in the early hours, just staring at the villa. It has made us wonder if he has anything to do with Mary's accident." Sam said.

"I should have mentioned it before, John, but I wasn't sure."

"Don't worry, Martha. I've seen him as well. I thought my mind was playing tricks on me. I can't understand how Mary fell over the cliff. It doesn't seem possible. I'm going to contact the police and get someone up here."

"Martha has already phoned. There is an officer searching outside."

"Great, I'll join him, after I've eaten. I'll take Alfie with me. I think we should cancel our bookings for today? It might be a good idea to stay indoors."

"Of course," Martha said.

"Yes, it's not safe." Eva agreed. "I'll start cancelling

the bookings and put some kind of sign up at the entrance. I'll say because of unforeseen circumstances the restaurant is closed until further notice."

"I'll give you a hand," Samantha said.

*

Outside the police officer was heading to the boathouse. John said he would come down and help him as soon as he had caught up with Alfie, who had run off into the bushes and was barking loudly.

"Come here, boy," he shouted. "Where are you?" John ran through the orchard, following the sound. Then the barking stopped. Alfie lay whimpering on the floor in a bush enclosure. John picked him up and tried to console him, but when John touched his stomach, Alfie yelped.

A sudden sound of crunching leaves interrupted John, and he watched as the dark silhouette of a young man hurried away. He knew the guy had kicked Alfie and anger swept through him.

"You bastard. I'm coming for you," he yelled. Scooping the spaniel up into his arms, he rushed back to the villa and laid the little dog in his basket.

Eva was in the kitchen and ran over to help.

"I think he's all right, but can you keep an eye on him it looks like he has been kicked in the stomach. I'm going back to help in the search. The guy has been spotted, so we need to get him."

"Of course, John, don't worry. I'll take care of Alfie."

John, now consumed with rage, was eager to continue his search. A short while later, he found the young man standing on top of the cliff. His posture gave the impression he was about to jump. Anger was swirling around in John's head. Visions of Mary and Alfie and the pain this boy had caused them added to his rage. He switched to his army training as he crept closer to the young man and watched his prey. His intention was to push him over the edge, but John hesitated for a second as the young man heard him and turned around. Startled by John's sudden appearance, he screamed like a wild animal and without warning jumped over the edge of the cliff to his death. For a moment, John stood frozen to the spot. His mind was back in Afghanistan, fighting for survival. His duty drummed into him to kill the enemy.

'Oh my God, what have I done?' The voices in his head, which he tried to keep under control, now yelled

back at him, "*He deserved to die. It wasn't your fault he was going to jump, anyway. After what he has done to Mary and Alfie, he had it coming to him. He was a total waster.'* But the thoughts didn't stop John from feeling remorse. If only he hadn't felt such anger, maybe he could have dealt with the situation differently and the boy might have lived. He pulled himself together. *'I didn't push him, he jumped'* the voices tried to reassure him as he rushed down to the beach to see where the young man lay. Alberto, the young police officer, was bent double. He was throwing up at the sight of the mangled body.

"Mi scuso," he said as he adjusted his uniform. He reached for his phone and alerted the police station to call off the search.

"Lo abbiamo trovato. Lui e morto. Si e suicidato" (*we've found him dead. He has committed suicide*). Alberto gave details of where they were and suggested a boat would be the easiest way to reach them.

John looked at the twisted body. Such a young man, he's only about 16 or 17. What a waste of a life. He felt a pang of regret as he took off his T-shirt and gently laid it

195

across the young man's face, which appeared strangely peaceful. As he did so, he recognized the silver necklace around the boy's neck. It was the one Mary always wore.

They both sat down to wait for the police back up to arrive, and quietness descended upon them. The gentle sound of the sea lapping on the sand helped to calm the situation. After a while, John phoned the villa to tell them the stranger was dead, and it was safe for them to go outside.

Samantha answered the phone and relayed the news to Eva.

"I should phone Franco and tell him," Eva said, as she reached for her mobile.

"Yes, he needs to know. Will you be all right if I go down to the beach to help John? I really need to do something."

"Of course, Sam, I'll let Martha know what is happening. She will be upset but relieved we are safe now."

"See you later," Sam said as she rushed out of the door and headed down to the beach.

"Franco, it's Eva. Can you talk?"

"Si, I'll step outside."

"We have something to tell you. Martha mentioned she had seen a young man hanging around the villa watching us. We've sent for the police. They have been searching for him and then John spotted him on the headland, but before he could stop him, the young man jumped off the cliff. They've found his body on the rocks. The thing is, we think he may have attacked Mary."

"Madre di Dio," (*mother of God*). "State tutti bene?" (*Are you all ok?"*)

"Yes, we are fine. How is Mary?"

"There are positive signs. The Doctor said a few minutes ago they want to take her off the machines, maybe today or tomorrow to see how she reacts. I was going to ring you. Perhaps you would come over? I'd like you to be here."

"Of course I'll come. Henrik is here. I'm sure he will give me a lift. I'll be with you soon. Try not to worry."

"Grazie, Eva," her father replied.

Eva headed for the kitchen. "Henrik, is there any chance of a lift to the hospital? I think Franco needs me

197

to be there."

"Of course. I'll meet you outside in ten minutes."

"Oh, that will be great. Thank you so much."

Eva headed upstairs to update Martha on John's news. She was resting on her bed with Alfie snuggled next to her.

"Poor John what a terrible thing to witness. I do hope he is all right. Is there anything I can do to help?"

"Not really, Martha. I've just spoken to Franco, and he said the doctors are hoping to take Mary off the machines soon. Henrik said he would take me to the hospital. I think someone should be there. We can't leave it all to Franco. Sam has gone down to the cove to help John. Will you be OK on your own?

"Yes dear, of course, I will. You get off and ring me as soon as you can. Be strong," Martha whispered to her. "I feel she is going to be fine."

*

Mary was clinging to life. The hospital had agreed Franco could stay with her as the police had confirmed she had no next of kin. This news had added to Franco's sadness and guilt. He sat by her side and whispered memories from their time together, praying she would remember him and respond. He had been so deeply in love that it didn't occur to him to ask about her upbringing. It was the moment Mary asked him about his family that everything went so wrong.

Now deep in his memories from years ago, Franco reflected on their last time together. Summer was almost over, and the moment had come to relax and wind down. They had driven to Positano, thrown their bags on the hotel bed, and headed for the beach before the sun disappeared. Neither of them had much time for sunbathing during the summer. Their jobs had been so busy.

Mary was relaxing on a sunbed. She was wearing a stunning bright red bikini, and she was well aware of its effect on him. He couldn't take his eyes off her.

"Maria, you are so beautiful. Tell me, why did you choose me to be your lover?"

She was quiet for a moment, considering the perfect answer.

"Well, Franco, it has to be your money. I guessed your secret a long time ago. You are not a tour guide, I think you own Capri, and I figure you are leading a double life. You want to experience what it is like to be ordinary."

He laughed. "Si, it is true. Do you see that motor boat over there?"

She looked over to where he was pointing and saw a beautiful streamlined boat moored in the water.

"It belongs to me. Come let's swim over. I'll show you around."

She jumped up and ran down the beach, leaving him behind. He watched as she swam in the boat's direction. As she approached the vessel, she waved to the people on board, and they beckoned to her and threw over a rope ladder. Laughing she clambered on board. A few moments later Mary stood on the deck, a glass of champagne in her hand, and she saluted Franco, who was standing open-mouthed, staring at her. Diving back into the water, she was soon by his side.

"You were lying! They've never heard of you!" she gasped as she sprayed him with water.

He put his arms around her and kissed her.

"You are the most challenging and exciting woman I have ever met. I love you with all my heart."

"I love you too," she said, pulling him closer to her. "Let's forget the sunbathing. I want you to show me how much you love me. Come on," and picking up their towels, they ran back to the hotel.

After a night in each other's arms, they woke the next morning to bright sunlight. Sitting on their terrace balcony, they drank in the sight and sounds of Positano, which lay stretched out in front of them like a picture postcard coming to life. Room service arrived and the aroma of hot coffee and warm pastries set their taste buds alive. Realising how hungry they were they didn't hesitate to tuck into the fresh delicacies.

After a leisurely breakfast they relaxed taking in the sun's warm rays and a peaceful feeling washed over them as they enjoyed each other's company without having to make conversation.

Mary moved to get her bag and pulled out a sketchpad and pencils. She began drawing, pointing out to Franco the colours of the magenta petals of the bougainvillea that were growing over the wrought ironwork on the balcony.

"Look how it compliments the colour of the green and

turquoise sea. Nature is quite remarkable."

Franco followed her gaze and was mesmerised by the beauty in front of him.

"Shall I show you my drawing?" Mary said, holding the picture close to her chest. He leaned over the table and took the sketchpad.

"You always amaze me." He laughed as he studied the nude drawing of himself.

"I believe I have captured your physique," Mary replied.

"I love it, Mary. It is very flattering, and it looks like me. You are so clever. May I keep it?"

"Of course, my darling. I hope forever."

As their weekend was almost at an end, Franco suggested having dinner in a restaurant in Montepertuso. She had heard of this tiny village high above Positano and always wanted to visit. They drove up the mountain road and arrived at a charming and traditional trattoria. The sun began its slow descent into dusk. Mary loved this part of the coastline. The splendour of Positano, with all its glittering lights, stretched below them. The small pastel-coloured houses covered in bougainvillea, majestically sweeping down to the darkening inky sea, were stunning. She couldn't take her eyes off the view. It just seemed magical. The reflections dancing on the water and the sounds of laughter and music all added to create a perfect setting.

"Grazie mille, Franco, for bringing me here. This is my favourite restaurant in the entire world. It's just beautiful."

"And so are you, Maria."

She smiled at him. "You Italians can certainly turn on the charm. I wouldn't put it past you to have arranged all of this just for me." She spread her arms out wide, encapsulating the entire view.

"As you said, Maria, I am extremely wealthy." He reached forward and touched her hand. "Let us enjoy the moment, shall we? I'll order some more wine. Shall we have a Prosecco to complement the Sicilian orange dessert?"

"That sounds delightful." She again turned her attention to the sight in front of her. "You are so lucky to have been born in such a beautiful part of the world."

"Ah, it's difficult living here. I have to work hard to

earn money. You would not believe some things tourists get up to. They get lost, miss the boat back from Capri, fall over, and end up in hospital." He sighed. "And, of course, families need feeding and taking care of. There is so much pressure."

He was hoping for some sympathy, but was taken aback by her reply.

"You have a family?" she enquired.

"Yes, of course, my mother, father, a brother, two sisters, Nonna and grandfather, oh and cousins–I have hundreds of cousins!"

"Oh I see, I thought for a moment you were going to tell me you were married with children." She laughed.

"No Maria," he hesitated, would now be the moment to tell her about his fiancé (the young Italian girl he was 'promised' to) "In Italy, it is different to England. We all live close to each other. We are honour bound, by the Church, to care for each other."

"Really? What, even in these modern days?"

"Well, more in southern Italy the family is everything in our culture and the mother is so important. She is the one who decides about our wellbeing. She makes her own pasta to make sure we don't go hungry! It is expected her children produce grandchildren for her to dote on."

"But what if you want to spread your wings and experience the world?"

"That's OK, so long as you come back one day to settle down and have children."

"Wow! I had no idea it was still like that. Have you told your parents about me?"

"My mother doesn't ask questions. If I'm happy she is."

Mary felt her mood slipping away. "Tell me straight, Franco. Our relationship, am I just a fleeting encounter in your life?"

"I don't understand Maria, what do you mean?"

She didn't mince her words. "Are we together as a couple? And are you intending to introduce me to your family, especially your mother? Or am I just another one of your many foreign girlfriends?"

The waiter arrived with the dessert, giving Franco a moment to gather his thoughts. He hadn't expected the conversation to take this turn.

The wine poured, Mary leaned over to Franco and stared into his eyes.

"Well, I need to know your answer."

"It's not that easy Maria, surely you must understand how much I love you."

"I thought I did, but I'm now wondering where we are going. I love you too. In fact, I've never experienced love like this, but if there is no long-term future for us then I'm not prepared to hang around and get more hurt every time I see you."

"Maria, don't say that please you are worrying me."

Mary became silent. The view, the music, the atmosphere was still the same … but she wasn't. She played with her dessert, and the silence between them became palpable.

The drive back to Sorrento along the famous romantic coastline was awkward. Franco was close to tears. How could he put this right? He could see how upset she was and that she needed an answer about their future. He wasn't sure himself and couldn't find the right words to express his feelings. Did he want to spend the rest of his life with her? Of course, he did, but there would be tears and tantrums from his mother. It would break her heart, but it would break his more if Mary disappeared from his life.

He stopped the car at the small apartment where she lived and took her hand.

"I'm sorry, Franco. I need some space. Thank you for a beautiful weekend."

"Oh, Maria." He tried to kiss her, but she pushed him away.

"We need a break. You are a grown man. I don't want to come between you and your family, but I have my pride and I won't be someone hidden away in the background. Goodnight."

She had walked away, and he hadn't tried to stop her. Tears streamed down Franco's face as the memory of their last meeting flooded back to him. He looked at Mary. Her body was a mass of wires linked to machines that made disturbing sounds. He held her hand.

"Maria, I love you so. Please, cara, please try to hold on. I'm here and I'm never going to leave you ever again." He heard a movement behind him and Franco, assuming a nurse was coming into the room, turned around.

Eva stood in the doorway, staring at him.

"Eva, Eva… wait, I can explain."

She had heard him declaring his love for Mary. Blinded by tears, she turned and rushed out of the building.

He wanted to go after her, but he would not leave Mary. He buried his head in his hands. How could he have caused so much unhappiness to the people he loved most in the world?

Eva stood at the entrance to the hospital, breathing in the warm air. Had she really overheard her father whispering words of love to Mary? It didn't make sense. They hadn't even met each other.

Henrik was waiting in the car park for her. As she walked towards him he could see she was crying. Fearing the worst, he got off his Vespa and rushed over.

"Oh, no. Is it Mary? She isn't dead, is she?" he asked.

Eva stared into the face of this young Danish man.

"No, no,"

"Eva, what has happened? Please tell me what is the matter?"

"I have to get away, Henrik. Please take me home."

"Of course. We can talk later."

The ride back to Sorrento was silent. Eva was so confused. None of what she had witnessed made any sense. Why would Franco be saying those things to Mary, and why was he crying?

When they had arrived back at the villa. Henrik helped her off his Vespa.

"Eva, please tell me what is troubling you. I want to help. I don't like seeing you so upset."

"Oh Henrik, you can't."

"Try me, I am an understanding guy."

"I saw Mary, and she was… oh, it was horrible… she was attached to machines and ... and Franco was holding her. I heard him whisper he loved her... had always loved her. He was willing her to wake up. When he saw I had come into the room, he was horrified. How can that be? They don't know each other. She kept making excuses to meet him when I asked her."

"Well, there is your answer. She must have met him. You said she lived here years ago. Maybe they were an item then?"

"What, Mary and my father? Oh, no. It's too much of a coincidence. She never said a word to me, even when I showed her the photograph of him."

Eva stared at Henrik.

"Oh my God, she recognised him from the photograph. I was so preoccupied with my own feelings to think anything of it. But, now I see, she was quiet and eager to get away."

"Eva, try not to jump to conclusions. You need more information."

"But he didn't remember my mother. Why should he remember Mary?"

"We have no idea what has happened. You need to speak to Franco. Try not to confuse things. It is not a competition for his love. Men are capable of deep love. They are not always good at expressing it to the people concerned besides, a love for a child differs from a love they have for their lover."

"But, I've only just found him!"

"Eva, you are experiencing such a lot of emotion. To find out the man you were told was your father, and it turns out he wasn't must have been an enormous shock.

But to find this exciting romantic foreign guy is your actual father, it's a lot to take in. What if he and Mary were husband and wife? You would have accepted the situation. It seems to me there is a triangle of tragic emotions going off. It is going to take time to process this, but the pieces will come together and everyone will be happy. Trust me."

"How come you are so wise?" She said to him and, calming down, gave an enormous sigh. "I'm over-reacting. I need to talk to him. It is dreadful what has happened to Mary."

"Good, I'm sure she is not trying to take Franco away from you. Mary is a straightforward person. She would not hurt you for the world."

Eva suddenly kissed him. "Thank you so much. I'm not sure how I would have coped without your help." She turned and headed for the restaurant, leaving Henrik staring after her. A smile spread across his face.

*

The following morning Eva and Samantha drove over to the hospital, after receiving a message from Franco to say that Mary was being taken off sedation.

"I'm dreading this Sam. Will she be OK, do you think?" Eva said.

"Don't worry, they know what they are doing. We just have to pray there is no long-term damage, anyway, we will soon find out." Samantha said as she drove into the car park.

After being given gowns and masks, the nurse allowed them into Mary's room. Franco was standing away from the bed as the medics attended to Mary. He was unaware of their presence.

Everyone was concentrating on Mary. The machine was beeping, and then it went silent. He moved closer.

"She's breathing on her own." The doctor said. "Hold her hand, Franco, and speak to her. It might help if she hears your voice."

He sat by her bed and whispered gently to her.

"Come on, Mary. It's Franco. Try to open your eyes. You are in hospital, but you are going to be fine." In Italian, he whispered words of love to her.

"Squeeze my hand, cara (darling). Sono qui" (I am here)."

She slowly responded and her eyes opened.

"She recognises me." He shouted to the doctor, who stepped forward.

"Mary, I am Dr Rossi. You have been in an accident, but you are doing very well. Can you speak?"

She took her gaze away from Franco. Her voice was weak but answered 'yes.' Then she spotted Eva.

"Eva?"

Franco turned and looked as Eva moved forward.

"I'm here for you, Mary, and so is my father. Try to rest, sweetheart."

Mary smiled and closed her eyes as her body relaxed and she drifted back to sleep.

"I think she is going to be OK. We'll monitor her very carefully over the next few hours." Dr. Rossi said. "She may sleep now for quite sometime. This is good. It will help her body heal."

Franco, his eyes filled with tears, turned to Eva.

"I didn't know you were here. Thank you for coming it means so much to me."

Eva moved forward to hug her father.

"Papa, you don't need to worry. It is obvious how much Mary means to you and it's wonderful you have found each other. I am thrilled for you both."

*

It had been two weeks since the attack on Mary. Dr Rossi was so encouraged with her progress and agreed to her being moved to a private hospital in Sorrento. Martha had insisted on paying for her care. She had settled in and Franco had been constantly by her side. There was a knock at the door.

"Hi Mary, it's me, Sam. Is it OK to come in?"

"Of course, it's so lovely to see you."

"It's a bit early in the day, but I wanted to see how you were settling in before we start work."

"I'm much better. It's nice here and the nuns, who are in charge, are so kind. I'm really happy to be nearer everyone too."

"Eva has sent you some delicacies she's made. They are savoury and sweet pastries."

"Oh, how thoughtful. Come and help me eat them."

"I was hoping you would say that." Sam pulled up a chair. "This is a lovely room and look at the view from your window, you can see all the Bay. Is that the villa in the distance?"

"Yes, I can keep my eye on you all," Mary laughed. She popped a pastry into her mouth. "Oh, they are gorgeous. The pastry is so buttery. Eva is such a talented girl."

"She is. This afternoon she has a booking for fifteen Italian women who want to celebrate a birthday. She persuaded them to have a traditional English tea party."

"Oh, they will love it. I wish I was there to see it."

"It's going to be fun. John is blowing up balloons and he's going to play some Frank Sinatra music to add some atmosphere. Martha is delighted. She's got her collection of English china out.

"Where is Franco?" Sam asked.

"I've sent him home. He is so tired. I told him not to come back until tomorrow, but I think he'll turn up tonight."

"He can't keep away from you. He has been so worried. We all think it is wonderful that you two are together again."

"Oh, that's nice to hear. Has Eva said anything?"

"She is delighted. At first, she was shocked that you knew Franco, but she now sees it as a bonus. You both get on well together. I guess it has all happened so quickly, but Eva and Franco seem to have an immediate bond. I wouldn't worry at all if I were you."

"It is such a relief to know that."

The door opened and sister Gabriella stepped in.

"Mi scusi signora non voglio disturbarla, ma il dottore Rossi è qui e vorrebbe una parola veloce" (Excuse me, ladies, I don't want to disturb you, but Dr. Rossi is here and would like a quick word.)

"Per favore, chiedigli di entrare." (Please ask him to come in) Mary said. "You don't mind, do you, Sam?"

Sam wiped the crumbs from her mouth and smoothed her hair. Mary hid a smile as she noticed how flustered Samantha had become.

"Buongiorno, Mary." Dr Rossi entered the room. His tall figure seemed to fill the doorway, and Sister Gabriella seemed to shrink in size.

"Dr Rossi, please come in. What a pleasant surprise. Do you remember Samantha?"

Sam stood up and smiled.

"Ciao signora. È così bello rivederti. ("hello. It is so nice to see you again.")

216

"Ciao Dr Rossi, è bello vederti anche tu." ("hello Dr Rossi, it's good to see you too")

She turned to Mary.

"Would you like me to wait outside?"

"No, no." Dr Rossi interrupted.

"It's a friendly visit. I was nearby and just wondered how you were and to make sure the Sisters of Mercy are treating you well." He winked at the nurse, who returned his smile.

"I'll leave you in peace, Doctor." She said as she closed the door.

"Well, Mary, you look comfortable. How are you?"

"Much better. I'm having physiotherapy on my leg and my headaches have almost gone."

"Such good news." He looked around the room. "I could stay here myself for a week or two, it's so pleasant." He spoke in English, so they both could understand him.

"I'm amazed at how hard you work. You must be exhausted, Doctor."

"It's our job. We are used to it."

"Did you know Samantha is an emergency nurse?"

"No, really?" He turned to face Sam.

"Yes, I worked in St Barts in London for ten years. I started my training there and worked up to being a senior nurse."

"I'm impressed. It is such a famous hospital. I had no idea you are a nurse."

"Yes, she has a lot of experience," Mary interrupted. "I'm hoping she is going to look after me when I leave here."

"I've spoken to your new doctor, and he said your brain scan shows how well you are healing. If you continue to improve, you may go home in four or five days. How do you feel about that?"

"I am so pleased. I'm sure Sam will monitor me and stop me from doing too much!"

"Of course I will. I know what you are like. You'll be going shopping and overdoing things, but I'll make sure you don't."

Dr Rossi reached into his jacket pocket. "Here is my card," he said as he handed it to Sam. "Any problems, I'm at the end of the telephone."

Sam graciously accepted his card.

"Now I can see my patient is in safe hands, I had better be getting back to the hospital."

"Before you go, Doctor, you must taste one of these pastries Eva has made for me."

"I had noticed them. I was hoping you would offer me one. He popped a pastry into his mouth. They are delicious. What a talent for someone so young."

"Dr Rossi, where are my manners?" Mary gushed. "As a thank you for saving my life, I would love to invite you and a guest to the villa for a delicious meal, my treat."

"How kind, I've heard so much about the restaurant. I would like that. I'm not married, so it will be just me."

Sam interrupted, "I'm not sure if Eva has told you, Mary, but we are making plans for a special evening to celebrate 'Farragusto' in two weeks. She has been going with Henrik into the mountains and experiencing traditional Italian food, like rich sausage and some amazing pork casseroles and bread. It will be a menu of traditional Italian food and wines.

"Does that suit you, Doctor?" Mary said.

"It sounds perfect, thank you."

"Great, Sam can phone you with the details."

He said goodbye. His eyes lingered on Sam for a few seconds. "So nice to meet you again."

After he had gone, Mary said. "He is nice and great looking, don't you think?"

"I do. You are lucky to have him as your doctor."

"I'd prefer him as a boyfriend," Mary laughed. "Anyway, how are things at the villa? Are Martha and John OK? I can't wait to see them."

"They will visit you soon. Martha has been anxious about you and when the young man killed himself she was so upset, although she tried to hide it. John has been brilliant. Did he tell you it was him and Alfie that found you on the cliff edge?"

"No, I remember very little about that day."

"When we realised you had gone missing, John looked for you. It was Alfie that alerted him. He sensed something was wrong, and he ran down the gorse bushes to the ledge and barked loudly until John came. You were in such a bad way, John rang the villa to get Franco to phone the emergency services and then he rushed down to help. Apparently, he instantly recognised you and stayed by your side all the time in hospital. He was

220

quite distraught, Mary. Nothing would reassure him until they brought you off the ventilator, and you started breathing normally. After that, he broke down in relief. He loves you so much."

Tears filled Mary's eyes. "I remember waking up and seeing Franco by my side. Then Eva came in and she looked so confused."

"It's been emotional for both of them, but the important thing is that you are getting better and you have found Franco. Eva has found her dad and they are getting on so well. She is very fond of you, Mary, even before she knew about you and her dad. Now she thinks it's all wonderful."

"Thank you, I'm so glad. I didn't want to come between them. I couldn't think what to do, so I went for a walk down to the cove to clear my head. I considered going back to England, but then I decided to tell Eva first before seeing Franco, to gauge her reaction. I was walking back up the hill and then I can't remember what happened. No wait, there was a noise, and I turned, and a young boy was rushing towards me. He looked angry. I can't remember anything after that."

"Oh, Mary how frightening for you. It was only after you were attacked we realised someone had been watching us. Martha and John had seen him hanging around the villa. The police said he had been living with the monks in the old monastery on the hill. They had taken him in, as he was homeless and very troubled. He stayed with them for sometime, coming and going, but then he disappeared."

"So what happened to him?"

"Well, the day after he attacked you. John had been looking around for any signs of the guy and found bits of blankets and food in the old boathouse. It looked like someone had been living there for some time. The police came just as the young man jumped from the cliff-top. John saw it happen and went to help but it was too late, his body was already lying on the rocks."

"Poor John, what an awful thing to happen."

"He is used to seeing things like that, Mary. The young Police Officer was pretty sick, though.

"Well, without John I don't think I would be here now. I owe him my life." Tears formed quickly in Mary's eyes and she changed the subject quickly.

"What about you Sam, how are you coping with everything?"

"I am much better although I can't deny it has been the worst thing losing Robbie. I've been so lost and alone. The villa and all of you have saved me. I am feeling normal again and I found the perfect place to scatter Robbie's ashes."

"Really! I've been so wrapped up in my own worries. You know I would have come with you if you wanted me to."

"I had to do it myself, so early one morning I went down to the cove, and I waited for the sun's rays to come through the rocks onto the sea. It was very beautiful and calm so I swam out and scattered his ashes on the water. I felt so incredibly peaceful. In my heart I knew that Robbie wanted to be set free so I could get on with my life, but at that moment, he was with me, and even now I know he is there if I need him. I often go down to the cove for a swim and just to be with him."

"Oh, Sam, it is such a beautiful place. I'm sure Robbie's spirit is there. I think I felt it that day when I decided not to go back to England."

Samantha smiled at Mary. "I think so too."

*

A few days later, Mary was allowed home with strict instructions to rest. Samantha had prepared her bedroom and decorated it with vases of sweetly scented flowers and pretty bed linen.

Franco helped her out of the car, treating her like a fragile sculpture. He then carried her up the stairs.

"I could get used to this treatment," she whispered to him as she wrapped her arms around him.

He kissed her tenderly. "I'm so pleased you are back, my darling. We have all missed you, and I promise to never let you out of my sight ever again."

Mary nestled her head in his neck. "I'm going to hold you to that."

She soon settled in and was overwhelmed with visitors popping in to wish her well. Alfie wouldn't leave her side, and it perturbed John that his affections were so fickle. But deep down, he was impressed with his little dog's empathy and Mary loved all the attention Alfie was giving her.

Signor Miccio arrived carrying an enormous basket of fresh fruit. He spent most of the afternoon regaling her with stories of his quest to find a rich woman who would take him away from the hard work he had endured over his life. She knew he was joking and everyone could hear her laughter all around the villa.

Martha also spent a lot of time with her. They chatted away and Mary was quite open about her upbringing and her childhood in care and foster homes.

"My dear child, I did not know how tough life had been for you. I admire you greatly. You have shown such resilience to hardship. It is wonderful that you and Francesco are together at last. Both of you deserve to be happy."

"I realised when I was young that life can deal you some bad cards, but I am stubborn and I will not allow myself to dwell on things."

"Quite right," Martha said, "and look where it has got you. You are your own person, and that is something few people achieve in their lifetime."

"I am lucky, Martha. To have had the opportunity to see a lot of the world and meet some amazing people,

225

and now Franco and Eva are in my life. I'm also extremely grateful for the day I met you. The villa feels like the home I've never had and I now have a family as well. I couldn't be happier."

"That fills my heart with joy, Mary. Anyway, my dear, shall we take a small walk around the terrace. Samantha has told me you need to exercise that leg of yours and Alfie is getting incredibly lazy these days."

Mary laughed. "She is an excellent nurse. She won't rest until I'm in the restaurant and back to work. As for Alfie, we have a lot in common. After all, he was abandoned once and now he has people around to love him."

*

The sound of the telephone echoed around the sitting room. John rushed to answer it.

"Pronto, si, un momento per favore."

"Anyone know where Martha is? There is a phone call from the monastery for her."

"I'll get her, John, she's just outside in the garden," Eva said.

A few moments later Martha appeared, pulling off her gardening gloves.

"It's the Abbott for you." John handed over the phone, and Martha settled herself in an armchair.

"Yes, that would be convenient." She spoke in Italian. "I will look forward to seeing him. Goodbye." Martha headed back to the kitchen.

"The Abbott is sending Brother Emmanuel to see me this afternoon. Apparently, the police visited them and there is some news about the young man."

Mary, who was sitting at the kitchen table carefully cleaning a pile of fresh vegetables, looked up. "I wonder what that's all about? Perhaps they've traced his family? It would be interesting to learn more about him. I can't get him off my mind."

"He is a mystery. Hopefully, Brother Emmanuel can shed some light on what was wrong with him." Martha said. "Mary, you take it easy and don't overdo it, dear."

"I'll be careful. It's so nice to be doing something and be part of the restaurant again." She smiled at Martha. "Don't worry, Eva is monitoring me."

Later that day Brother Emmanuel arrived at the villa on

an ancient, worn-out bicycle.

"Please come in, it is so nice to meet you." Martha led him into the sitting room.

"Can I get you some refreshments? Perhaps you would join me in a cup of tea?"

"Yes thank you, that would be most agreeable." Brother Emmanuel said as he eased himself into a comfy armchair.

A few minutes later Samantha arrived carrying a tray with a china teapot and matching crockery, together with a plate of freshly baked scones, jam, and cream. Brother Emmanuel's eyes lit up.

"After all my time living in England," Martha said, "I still enjoy a nice cup of tea and scones in the afternoon."

She passed him a plate and was delighted to see him tuck in with a hearty appetite.

"The Abbott said you've heard from the police about the stranger?"

"Yes, Signora, apparently they traced him to a young girl who reported him missing. She is his sister and told a very sad tale. His name is Giovanni and was from a very poor part of Naples. His father, who, apparently abused the family, disappeared recently after he had gone fishing in his old boat and never returned. The police had been investigating him regarding the abuse he had caused his family, and they closed the case, assuming he had drowned himself." Brother Emmanuel hesitated for a moment to take a sip of tea. "A short while later, his young son, Giovanni, also went missing. His sister said that since the disappearance of their father, her brother had become distraught. They couldn't cope with his behaviour. He refused to speak to them and exhibited some kind of breakdown. Her mother became quite frightened of him."

"What an awful situation," Martha said. "The mother and daughter how are they now?"

"Coping well, life is much easier for them. They continue to sell the jewellery they make in the street market and now they can keep the money without the father taking it."

"Oh dear, what a terrible life. We shouldn't make assumptions, but I wonder if Giovanni had anything to do with his father going missing?"

"It may be, Signora. When he arrived homeless at the

Monastery, we learned nothing from him, although he seemed to find some kind of peace with us, but one day he started experiencing psychotic behaviour, and then he ran away. He had many scars on his body and we presumed he was self-harming. In retrospect, we all agree we should have helped him more, but we hoped he would settle down."

"What happened to his body? Was he buried in Sorrento?"

"The authorities agreed we could lay him to rest in the monastery graveyard. The family couldn't afford a funeral and we felt it was the least we could do."

"It is reassuring to know he was treated in such a kind way. It is a terrible thing that has happened to Mary and needs addressing, but it sounds like he was not in his right mind and, from what you said, his father may have been responsible for the way he behaved."

"Yes, indeed. I'm afraid there is no more I can tell you, I must make my way back. Thank you for your hospitality, Signora."

"Thank you, Father, I'll show you the way out."

John watched the elderly monk struggle to get on his

bicycle, and rushed to offer him a lift back in his car. Brother Emmanuel gratefully accepted. The tea and scones had made him somewhat sleepy, and the idea of pedalling up the rough track back to the monastery was something he wasn't looking forward to.

When John returned, Martha related the news to them all. Mary sat quietly until she had finished speaking.

"How awful, such a terrible life. I just don't understand why he picked on me, though. It wasn't as though he knew me."

"I have a theory," John said. "When we found his body, he had a silver necklace around his neck. I think it was yours, Mary. I wonder if he saw you buy it and followed you. His sister or his mother probably made it. Do you remember the creepy guy in the restaurant who you said stared at your chest? Well, it could have been him and he saw the necklace and recognised it. When the opportunity came, he pushed you over and took it off you."

Mary shuddered at the thought.

"Interesting theory, John, but we will probably never find out for certain," Martha said.

231

Mary agreed. "Now I understand more, I can make sense of it. I can even feel sorry for him. He had such an awful life."

"You may have been a victim of being in the wrong place at the wrong time," Samantha said as she moved over to where Mary was sitting to give her a reassuring hug.

*

Ferragosto
(Italian Holiday)

Eva was busy preparing her menu of traditional food for the Ferragosto celebrations. John had hired two young musicians to play the guitar and sing popular Neapolitan songs. He had decorated the restaurant with swathes of greenery, flowers, and fairy lights. Martha was the first to appear, looking as elegant as ever. She loved a party, and Ferragosto was such a special Italian celebration. Determined to enjoy every second, she didn't hesitate to offer a welcoming smile to all the diners and guests. Sam wandered around carrying trays of drinks, but her eyes were fixated on the drive.

"Is there any sign of him?" Mary asked.

"Who?" Sam replied.

"Dr Rossi. You invited him, didn't you?"

"Yes, of course, when he phoned to check on you. I reminded him. He said he was looking forward to it. Perhaps he has been delayed at the hospital."

"I'm sure he will come. I got the impression he wanted to see you again." Mary said.

"Oh, I don't know about that."

Mary smiled to herself. *'She does like him. I knew it!'*

"Well, we won't have to wait long. I think he's just arrived." Mary said as she pointed to an open-topped sports car turning into the parking area. Sam, with a welcoming smile, walked towards him.

"Dr Rossi, I'm so pleased you came."

"Please, Samantha, call me Lorenzo. I must apologise for being late. I had difficulty leaving the hospital."

"You are here now, that is all that matters. Would you like some food and a glass of wine? And would you care to join the others? They are at the long table, under the terracing. I am still helping with the guests, but I'll be with you soon."

"Grazie," he said, smiling.

"Dr Rossi, please come and join us," Mary said as she stood to welcome him. "Let me introduce you to Martha. She is the amazing lady who has made all this possible for us."

Mary spread her arms to encompass the restaurant.

"Signora, I am delighted to meet you. Mary has told me a lot about you."

"Grazie, but it is my pleasure. I have been waiting for the chance to thank you for saving and caring for Mary."

"It's my job, and there was a team of people working on her. It was a relief when she regained consciousness."

"Ah, here comes John and Eva with some food. I hope you are hungry!" Martha said.

"I am Signora. I've only had a snack all day."

There was an impressive selection of meats, including slow-cooked porchetta (pork), spicy sausages, carpaccio, rabbit stew, succulent spit-roasted chicken, pasta, frittata, a variety of bread, pizza slices dripping in hot oil. The fragrance of garlic, basil, and rich tomato sauces, filled the air. Cheeses, figs in mascarpone and maple syrup, Sfogliatelle (flaky pastries) together with fresh whole peaches in iced red wine completed the platter. Lorenzo, his eyes lighting up, tucked into his food.

"This is such a delight. It brings back memories of my dear nonna's cooking."

"How wonderful. I remember my grandmother and my mother's food. They spent so much time and love on preparing their dishes, just like Eva does." Martha agreed.

"Signora, she is a very talented young lady. She has an intuition for Italian food."

Franco joined in the praise. "She has and don't forget she is half Italian, so she must have inherited it from me! I am so proud of her."

A short while later, Samantha appeared. She had changed from her waitress uniform into a flattering pale pink dress and seated herself next to Lorenzo.

"Are you enjoying your evening?" she asked.

"Marvellous, everyone has been so kind, and the food was special to me. Tonight has made me realise I don't socialise enough. The villa has a wonderful atmosphere."

"Yes, music is part of the dining experience. We like to get people up and dancing and often improvised singing! Would you like me to show you around?"

"Si, Si, I would love that."

"Follow me, I'll give you a guided tour."

They entered the kitchen, and Lorenzo could see Eva had everything under control. She welcomed them with open arms.

"So this is where all the wonderful food comes from. Signorina, your cooking is superb. My nonna would have been impressed."

"How wonderful. it's very kind of you to say. Grazie.

I'm so pleased you enjoyed it. I'm learning a lot about Italian cuisine. Let me introduce you to Henrik he is my right-hand man, and he is teaching me Danish cookery as well."

Henrik moved forward, extending his hand in welcome. They chatted for a while, and then Samantha showed Lorenzo around the villa.

"Such an amazing house. I would love to live here." He said as he looked at the magnificent ceilings and chandeliers.

"I know, so very different from my humble beginnings in London." Sam smiled; she was relaxing in his company. "Let me show you the roof terrace? The views are amazing."

He followed her up the stone staircase out onto an enormous roof space which was furnished with swing seats, loungers, and coloured umbrellas.

"As the restaurant grows, we will do something with this area. We are not short of ideas, but at the moment we use it as a private place to come if we want to relax." The sound of distant fireworks interrupted Sam. "Oh, isn't that beautiful?" The sky lit up with sparkles and colour and they both stood close to each other, watching the display over the Bay.

"It's perfect," he said, turning to face her, his eyes lingering for a moment. He was enjoying seeing the delight, which was written all over her face.

"Fireworks always make you remember when you were a child, don't you agree?"

"I was just thinking the same thing."

They stood together soaking up the atmosphere as the fireworks continued to light up the bay and sky.

"Shall we go back and join the others?"

"Yes, of course. It has been so enjoyable seeing the villa. I can understand why it is important to you all. It is really a beautiful place."

As the evening wore on, the music became more romantic and it encouraged diners to take to the dance floor. Franco was clutching Mary to him in a slow dance. Martha was also dancing with Signor Miccio, who was clasping her tightly. Sam and Lorenzo settled in a secluded area and enjoyed the variety of desserts and champagne, which John had brought over. They became deep in conversation, and soon they were learning a lot about each other. Sam was trying hard to avoid discussing Robbie, but it was inevitable he would crop up in their conversation. It saddened Lorenzo to hear her story.

"We have a lot of patients and their families who go through such tragedies. Sometimes I find it hard to cope with their sorrow. This is the major reason I became a doctor. To cure people was my desire. But, of course, that does not always happen. You need time to grieve, I'm sure one day you will be happy again."

Sam smiled. "Being here has helped me. It's hard to feel sorrow when you are surrounded by beauty and sunshine. It has been a healing process - time to recover. I'm just taking each day as it comes and now I've laid Robbie to rest here, I feel a tremendous sense of relief. He really loved Sorrento and I feel close to him."

"Do you imagine you will go back to nursing again?"

"I hope so. When Mary was in hospital, it has made me realise I am ready, but I am enjoying being part of this venture and, in my heart, I feel more like myself again. Does that make sense?"

He reached for her hand. "It makes perfect sense.

Samantha, would you care to dance?"

"I would love to," she said as he led her to the dance floor.

*

THE SUMMER ENDS

(L'estate finisce)

The end of the season arrived. The restaurant had been emerging over the summer to become one of Sorrento's finest. Then the tourists went home, and the weather changed. Rain, thunder, lightning illuminated the skies. The hot summer had turned into autumn. Bookings for the restaurant slowed down. The tourists were going home having had a fabulous holiday and determined to return next year. One Saturday evening at the end of October, Martha asked everyone to join her in the sitting room. The room was full of the scent of pine logs blazing in the fireplace, giving warmth and comfort against the dark and threatening skies outside.

"Come in, get nice and comfy. I just wanted a chat with you all. First, I want to say how much I appreciate all your hard work in making the restaurant such a success. My villa has been brought back to life, and it is you I want to thank. I was so delighted when you all agreed to come and live with me. It is all down to your love and hard work that it is such a success."

John interrupted. "Honestly, Martha, you gave us all a wonderful opportunity. It should be us thanking you."

"That is kind of you to say, John, and I appreciate it.

But I wanted to discuss the winter. The holiday season is drawing to a close, so I don't know what your plans are. I want you to know this will always be your home."

"The thought of winter is unbearable," Eva said. "I'm just getting going, it's so much fun."

"Well," Martha continued. "I saw my solicitor last week, and he informed me my house in London has sold very well, and with George's investments, I can say that I am a very wealthy woman and I have made provision in my Will to leave the villa and restaurant to you all equally. Of course, I don't intend to go anywhere yet, but I needed to make sure that your future is secure."

There was a stunned silence. Mary was the first to speak.

"Martha, that is unbelievably kind of you."

"Please, Mary, it is my deepest wish. In the future, you may decide to move on to new things. If that happens, there is a clause in my Will, which enables you to buy each other's share. It is all legal and rather technical. The important thing in my mind is that I cannot take it with me. I would hate the villa to go back to the neglected state it was when we came here. There is no one else I would want to leave it to. I also want to invest more into the villa. I've listened to John, who has some exciting ideas. First, to get the vineyard up and running and hope to harvest a good crop of grapes so we can produce our own wine one day. It may take some time, but I do agree it will be an asset. I would like to extend the gardens and grow more fruit and vegetables, especially to harvest the olives and turn them into good oil. I am sure Eva will agree that this is important."

Sam and Mary looked at each other and then glanced at Eva, who had tears streaming down her face.

"I just can't think of the future. This place would not be the same if you were not here." She said, wiping away her tears.

"Eva, darling, when my time comes, I will be with my beloved husband. I realise I have been so blessed. My life has been wonderful, but I have no intention of going anywhere yet. There is far too much work to do here."

Samantha, who had been sitting quietly, said. "I think this might be a good time to tell you my news. The hospital in Sorrento has offered me three day's work. Lorenzo suggested it to them. It will just be over the winter, and I can help here during the rest of the week. When Mary was in the hospital, I realised how much I had missed nursing. This arrangement would allow me to do both if everyone agrees. The restaurant is something I love. You have all helped me get through such a tough time. All the fun and laughter has been the best possible medicine."

"You must take the offer, Sam," Martha said. "Your experience shouldn't be wasted and I'm sure the hospital will be grateful to have your knowledge."

"Thank you, Martha. I'm looking forward to trying it. My intention is to carry on in the restaurant during summer. I can't imagine not being part of this place and I can't thank you enough for the kind gift you have just given us."

Martha, with a big smile on her face, turned to John.

"Would you mind getting us some drinks? I think this calls for a toast to celebrate all our futures."

*

As autumn turned to winter and the weather became cold, the villa took on a new life form. They stored away tables and chairs from the outdoor restaurant. The tourists and diners had gone, and a strange feeling of quietness descended on the building. Eva was busy experimenting with new recipes and, with Henrik's help; they set up a daily blog about creating an Italian restaurant in southern Italy. They knew social media was the place to get the villa noticed, and it was going well receiving a lot of 'hits.'

Her relationship with her father became a constant source of happiness. In her spare time, she would go down to Marina Grande with Henrik, to help Franco restore his boat. They were happy days messing about with painting and varnishing. Henrik had taken a genuine interest in the boat, which delighted Franco. The anticipation of taking her out on the sea was something they were all looking forward to.

Franco was trying hard to make up for her early up-bringing without him, and she had to keep reminding him to relax. She knew he would always be there for her, and she couldn't have wished for a better father. What Eva hadn't expected, when she planned her trip to Italy to find him, was to discover romance as well. She loved being around Henrik. They had naturally bonded together, enjoying the same sense of humour and also a love of cooking. His gentle personality and happy disposition attracted everyone to him. The kitchen was always full of laughter and made everyone smile.

On a lovely bright evening in November, they rode out to the hills of St Agata. Snuggled together on a swing seat outside their favourite bar, they watched the sun slip below the sea, sending rippled colours of Mediterranean fruits across the sky.

"I shall miss this when I go back to Denmark," Henrik said.

"Don't go," Eva replied softly. "I don't want you to go."

Henrik put his arm around her. "Really, you want me to stay with you?"

"Of course, I do. There is no need for you to go, is there?"

"Well, I have a job lined up for the winter in my father's business, but it's nothing special. I'm sure he can manage without me. Although they want me home for Christmas and the New Year. My mother is constantly asking when I'm coming back. She misses me! Trouble is, as much as I love my family, I also love it here ... with you."

Eva's face lit up with pleasure. "Wow! I'm so glad you said that. It would be awful if you weren't here. I would miss you so much. You know, I'm sure Martha will let you stay in the villa; there's lots of room. We can plan how to move forward with the restaurant next year."

"Brilliant, I would really like that. If Martha agrees, then I would love to stay. I need to earn some money, though. Will there be enough work?"

"There is a lot of work to do, especially planting crops and redecorating the rooms ready to let them out next season. You don't need to worry. There is more than enough work for all of us during the winter."

"What are your plans for Christmas, Eva? I wonder if you would like to come to Copenhagen to visit my family? They are eager to meet you, and I could show you what Denmark is like."

"I would love to, but I can't come for Christmas. It is my first one with my father, and I would feel awful leaving Martha after all she has done for me. Perhaps, I could fly over and join you for the New Year? What do you think? It will be something to look forward to."

"I understand. Maybe I'll stay for Christmas too. I'll tell my parents we are coming over in time for New Year? I'm sure they will be happy with that, especially if I am bringing my beautiful English girlfriend with me. My mother will be delighted." He put his arm around her. They moved closer to each other as they watched the last moments of the sun slip below the horizon and their kisses sealed their future.

*

The days passed more slowly now the restaurant was closed. Everyone had slipped into their own routines, enjoying time off, but also getting on with the work in the villa. Mary continued to make a good recovery. Her relationship with Franco and Eva grew day by day.

"What are you two whispering about?" Mary said. They were both talking in the kitchen.

"Franco was telling me about his lugger boat. Did you know the new sails have arrived?"

"No, I didn't. What colour are they?"

"Deep terracotta. Can you imagine them against the turquoise sea? It will look amazing, don't you think?"

"Yes, I can't wait to go sailing. We must take Martha for a trip out, Franco? She will love it. I bet it has been a long time since she has been sailing around Capri."

"Yes, we could all go. The boat is almost ready. A little more work, but as soon as the weather is good enough we shall try it out while it is nice and quiet. We can have the place all to ourselves."

"Great idea. Now I'm going for my daily walk. Does anyone care to join me?" Mary said.

"You go, Franco. I have something I need to do," Eva replied.

"OK, Signora, where are we headed today?"

Franco took Mary's arm, and they walked out into the cool air, with Alfie trotting happily behind them.

"I think you need a change of scenery, Mary," Franco said as they walked around the gardens. "Tomorrow, after work, I shall come and take you for a drive. Does that sound good to you?"

"I would love that. Where shall we go?"

"Ah, wait and see. It will be a pleasant surprise."

True to his word, Franco arrived at midday. He couldn't help but feel immense pride as he opened the car door for her. She had decided it was time to dress up in one of her favourite outfits. It had been ages since she had been anywhere. Going through her wardrobe, she chose a midi orange woollen dress and boots. A black jacket draped over her shoulders and designer sunglasses completed her outfit. She looked like a film star.

"I didn't know what to wear today. The sun is still warm but the evenings get quite cold, don't they?" she said.

"Cara, you look perfect."

"Thank you, and you are very smart yourself. I'm so excited to be going out. Where are we headed?"

"I'm not telling you," he said. "Sit back and relax. Enjoy the scenery."

He drove at a leisurely pace through the hills and on to the Amalfi coast road. Mary had travelled this road many times, and yet it was like seeing it for the first time. A soft mist hung over the mountains, sending delicate lavender streaks of light cascading down to the sea.

A feeling of joy filled Franco's heart as he relaxed into the drive. He had his Maria back, and all was well with the world. He hummed, which led to an Italian love song.

Mary sat spellbound.

"Wow, Franco. I didn't know you could sing. Your voice is gentle but so emotional. I love it."

"There is a lot you don't know about me, Mary."

"I'm realising that, my darling. I can't wait to find out more."

They drove through the small town of Positano, the road enticing them on towards Amalfi.

"Oh, I love this area. It looks like a picture postcard. Aren't we stopping?"

"Maybe on the way back. I'm taking you to a special place, but we need to be there at 2 pm."

"I'm intrigued."

Fifteen minutes later, they parked on the roadside. Mary looked around and then she spotted the worn-out sign 'Grotto Delle Smeraldo.'

"How fabulous," Mary cried out. "The Emerald Grotto in Amalfi. Oh, Franco, I've always wanted to visit but never managed it."

"Andiamo," he said as he held her hand and led her to an old lift. "We could go down the steps, but I'm worried about your leg. I don't want you to slip, so hold me tight."

They descended from the lift and reached the entrance to the grotto, which was dark and wet.

"Ciao Peppino." Franco greeted his friend.

"Ciao Franco. It's been a long time."

"Mary, let me introduce you to my dear friend, Peppino. He is going to let us borrow his boat."

"Ciao," Mary said as she went straight in for a hug. "I'm so excited to be here."

"Ah, signora, it is a pleasure to meet you. You have the boat all to yourselves. Franco, I trust with my wife, and daughters and my precious boat. Here, Franco, it is all yours."

Mary stepped into the wooden structure. It was more like a raft than a boat. Soon they emerged into the grotto. The water was a fantastic, luminous shade of green. She trickled her fingers into the sea. Droplets of water trickled off her hand like hundreds of tiny emeralds. The sheer beauty of the cavern mesmerised her.

Franco pointed out the stalagmite structures rising from the seabed.

"Look at the vaulted ceiling and the stalactites. This is

where the drops of water come from. It has taken over a thousand years to create this scene, just for you."

They listened to the gentle drips of water and the soft movement of the emerald green sea.

"It is so magical. I love it in here. I feel we have escaped the world into a paradise." Mary said as she again trickled her fingers into the water.

Franco rowed the boat over to a safe spot to stop so they could take in the grotto's magnificence.

"Maria," he said as he reached for her hand. "Marry me?"

"What did you say?"

"Marry me?"

She held his hand and stared into his eyes, her voice strong and genuine as she replied.

"Yes, yes, yes."

He laughed as he handed her a tiny leather box. She opened it, her eyes wide. Delight was etched on her face as she saw her engagement ring.

"Oh, Franco, it is so beautiful."

He took the ring and placed it on her finger. It was a perfectly formed square emerald set in a delicate gold setting.

"I chose it because it is the colour of your eyes."

They stayed for a while, enjoying their moment together.

"Andiamo cara. We must get the boat back to Peppino before he gets worried."

"I shall remember this moment all my life. Thank you for making me so happy."

He kissed her passionately. "Now for the next part of our day."

Back in the car, they headed to Amalfi, but Franco didn't stop there, instead, he took the long winding road up to the hills to Ravello.

They just made it in time for a quick visit to the famous Villa Rufolo. Wandering hand in hand through the gardens and out to the terrace to see the world-famous spectacular views.

"Next summer we will come back and listen to the outdoor concerts. It is a wonderful experience to listen to opera under the stars and with the Tyrrhenian Sea as a backdrop. You will love it." Franco said as he gazed across the awe-inspiring view.

"It would be lovely if we could bring everyone. Martha will enjoy it, especially with her love of opera and theatre. It must be years since she has been here."

"Of course. Eva and Henrik could come. I think the two of them are getting quite close."

"Just like a father trying to marry his daughter off."

"I like him. He is a good person and I think he will make her happy and give me lots of grandchildren. I could teach them to fish and sail."

Mary laughed. "Come on, I'll buy you a coffee." They headed for the market square.

"Goodness everywhere is so quiet now the tourist season is over," Mary said as she sipped her hot drink.

"Indeed. Isn't it wonderful? It all belongs to the Italians again."

As they drove back along the coast road, Mary settled in her seat. She felt so relaxed, and her thoughts drifted to the moment Franco had proposed. She gazed at her ring.

"Franco, it would have been so funny if you had dropped the ring in the emerald grotto."

"Did you say funny?"

"Yes, would you have dived in and searched for it?"

"It had crossed my mind if such a terrible thing were to happen. I know you would have insisted I jumped in."

Her finger touched the stone. "You are right. I would have pushed you in. Thank goodness it is on my finger."

He smiled at her, so happy in the moment. He didn't want this day to end, and neither did Mary.

They headed back to the car and upon reaching Positano, she noticed Franco take a turn up the mountain road.

"Are you hungry? Shall we stop for a meal? There is a nice little place that serves delicious food just up this road."

"Ah, I know where we are going. It's the Trattoria in Montepertuso?"

"Si, you are right. I thought it was time to erase a terrible memory and replace it with a good one."

Her heart was beating fast as they parked the car outside the restaurant. The sun was setting, filling the sky with glorious orange streaks.

"It hasn't changed. I can't believe it has been twenty years since we came here."

Franco guided her to the same table overlooking the terraced hillside towards Positano. The fairy lights, which adorned the trelliswork, danced in the early evening dusk. Local people were filling the restaurant, and an atmosphere of gaiety and laughter rang out. Their meal was delicious. Mary chose a beefsteak and Franco, spaghetti alle vongole, washed down with the local wine. The waiter appeared to clear the table, and Mary noticed a nod between him and Franco. Suddenly the owner appeared carrying a birthday cake.

"Oh, you remembered." She cried in delight.

"How could I ever forget this date? For years I have spent your birthdays wondering if you remembered me."

"I never forgot you, Franco, and I am so sorry I reacted the way I did. I've always loved you and ..." she stopped, tears running down her face.

"Mary, I was as much to blame. I was young and torn between you and my family."

Riccardo, the owner, looked confused.

"Hey, you don't like the cake?"

She looked at him and in Italian said. " I love the cake. It is the best cake in the whole world, especially as this is such a special moment for us. We are getting married," she cried out.

The diners cheered as Riccardo lit the candles, and shouts of congratulazioni and Buon Compleanno filled the room.

As they drove back towards the villa. Franco stopped the car on a dirt track.

"Maria, don't go back to the villa tonight. Stay with me. Come to my home."

"I would love to," she replied.

He put the car into first gear and in a cloud of dust they headed to Marina Grande.

*

Mary arrived home the following morning. She was glowing with happiness.

"Come and look at Mary," Sam said as she observed Franco open the car door for her. "They can't stop laughing."

Eva joined her. "My dad said he was planning something special for her birthday. I hope he proposed."

"Come on," Sam said as she grabbed Eva's arm.

"Martha," Eva shouted up the stairs. Mary's back."

"I'll come down, dear."

"Well," Martha said, as she greeted them both. "Did you have a nice birthday?"

"I had the most wonderful day," Mary said as she waved her hand around to display the sparkling emerald on her finger. Squeals of delight filled the hallway.

"Oh, such wonderful news. Congratulations to you both." Martha hugged them.

Alfie ran into the room. He could sense all the excitement in the air and he joined in, his tail wagging happily. John was close behind him.

"Have I missed something?"

"It's celebration time. Mary and Franco are engaged."

"Congratulations, this is the best news." John shook Franco's hand and went to hug Mary.

"Come and sit down and tell us all about your day," Eva said.

"I'm not sure where to start? It was wonderful from start to finish."

"Mary, I'm sorry, but I have to go to work." Franco interrupted. " I'm late. Shall I come tonight?"

"Yes, of course, you must go. I'll see you later. "

"Come for dinner. We will celebrate." Eva said to her father. "I'm so happy for you both."

Franco kissed his daughter on the cheek. "That pleases me greatly."

*

A couple of weeks later, on a wet afternoon, Mary and Franco were discussing their wedding plans.

"I just want to marry you, now." he said. "I can't wait any longer."

"Me too, darling. Next summer seems a long way off, and I agree with you, a quiet intimate affair would be lovely."

Martha, who was sitting close by suggested, "Why don't you get married here? We could fill the villa with flowers and candles. Light all the fires to give warmth and prepare lots of lovely food? We will make it a real celebration."

"That sounds wonderful. What do you think, Franco?" Mary said.

"Yes, this is the perfect place, and after we could slip away for a few days' honeymoon, maybe Venice?"

"It sounds amazing." Her face lit up with delight. "Venice is a place I have always wanted to visit."

"You've never been to Venice? Mamma Mia, you will love it. I can't wait to show you. Martha, tell her how wonderful it is."

"Everyone should see Venice. Many years ago George and I went on holiday. We stayed in a fine hotel on the Grand Canal during the carnival in February." She smiled as her memory of George came to her mind. "He fell in love with it until we wandered around late at night and people jumped out at us in the dark alleyways. Everyone dresses up in elaborate masks. They wear the most exciting costumes, but the masks frightened him somewhat."

"How funny, Martha. From everything you told us about George, I can't imagine him being afraid of anything." Mary said. "I love hearing stories about him. It would have been wonderful to have met him."

"Ah, how marvellous that would have been. I know he would have loved you all." She said wistfully as her memories again crowded into her mind. "Anyway, going back to your wedding. What do you think about the villa as your venue? Of course, we will have to get a license." Her mind started racing again. "I can't believe we hadn't thought of it earlier. We could open it up for weddings next year. It is the perfect setting. It would add another string to our bow and would be an exciting venture."

"It certainly would Martha. We could be the trial run. Who shall we invite, Franco? All my friends are here. There is no one else I would like to ask. Are there people you would like to join us?'

"I'm not sure. I have some close friends I would like to invite. My sisters are in the US with Luca so I don't think they will be able to come."

"Has anyone seen John today? Martha said. 'I'll run it past him, see if he likes the idea of the villa becoming a wedding venue."

"He is in his workshop, working on his projects." Mary replied."

"Goodness, he spends a lot of time in there."

Franco laughed. "John is enjoying making his leather goods again. A man needs somewhere to escape to, especially from so many women in the house."

"And where are you going to escape to?" Mary asked.

"My boat, of course. One day it will be finished, and I will sail around the islands showing off. I might even let you come with me."

Mary smiled. "Of course I'll be sailing with you. I wouldn't miss that for anything."

"I think I'll go and get him. It would be nice to have his views," Martha said as she reached for her walking stick.

"Don't worry, Martha, I'll go. I'm curious to see what he is up to." Mary replied. "I won't be long."

For the last couple of hours, John had been pacing up and down in his workroom. A mood had descended on him, and he was struggling to shake it off. His past episodes of depression had eased recently. The excitement of a new venture had filled his thoughts, and being part of a group of people made him feel less alone in the world. Now the season had ended, he'd found he had more time on his hands …time to think.

'*I just need to focus, get a grip on the present, and put the past behind me,*' his inner voice repeating the same mantra. But it wasn't working.

A knock at the door brought him back to reality.

"John, are you in there?" It was Mary.

For a moment he considered ignoring her, but he straightened his back and with a forced smile on his face he shouted. "Yes, come in Mary."

"Hope I'm not disturbing you. Just wanted a quick chat. Franco and I have been discussing a wedding venue and Martha came up with a brilliant idea to have it here. Of course, that would mean getting permission to conduct wedding ceremonies. Well, one thing led to another and now she wonders how you would feel about the villa becoming a wedding setting next year, for guests. When the bedrooms are refurbished, we can accommodate twenty-plus people. What do you think?" John stared at her.

"Are you OK, John? Don't you think it is a good idea? I know it's a lot of extra work, but we can take on more staff. It would be brilliant for the restaurant, too."

"Of course, it is an excellent suggestion. Sorry, Mary, I was miles away."

"You don't seem yourself? Are you sure you are feeling all right?"

John slumped into a chair. "I just feel a bit low at the

moment. You know it's the PTS thing. Sometimes it just hits me. I'm better off on my own, try to get my head sorted."

"Oh, John, I'm so sorry I didn't realise." Mary sat down next to him. "Look, would it help to talk? Do you know what has triggered it? Maybe I can help?"

"Thanks, Mary, that's kind of you, but I don't see how you can. It's difficult to explain. I don't understand it myself."

"Try me. Is it about your time in Afghanistan? I'm a good listener you know."

John put his hands to his face. He was struggling to control his emotions.

"I just keep seeing faces and hearing voices and I can't make it go away."

"Who are the faces, John?" Mary whispered gently.

"People I've killed! Their eyes haunt me. They won't let me rest …and my mates who were blown up …and then there is him!"

"Who, John?"

"The young man, of course, the one who pushed you."

"But why is he in your head?"

"I saw him, Mary. I was so enraged. He was standing on the cliff edge and I crept up behind him. I was going to push him over." John's voice rose sharply as the memory overwhelmed him. "He must have heard me, and turned around and there it was that same look of fear in his eyes when he knew I was after him… and then he jumped … to his death!"

Mary reached for John's hand.

"But it wasn't your fault. Giovanni was mentally disturbed. If anyone is to blame, it's his father who abused the young lad throughout his life. Like the other faces, you see they are the enemy and you have been trained to kill them. I can't understand how that feels, but your intentions were right. You mustn't beat yourself up about it, John. To be honest, if it had been me on that cliff, I would have pushed him off as well. By all accounts, his mother and sister have suffered at his hands. They didn't deserve this treatment, and I didn't either. I was nothing to him. In his twisted mind, he saw the necklace and wanted it. Not to remind him of his sister, but he didn't want me wearing it. It's a control thing and thankfully I survived and I've forgiven him.

My start in life was terrible, John. My mother abandoned me as a baby, chucked out, unloved, not wanted, but if I had allowed it to I think it would have ruined my life. I can't keep anger inside me when I don't know the reasons, so I've moved on. It's all about forgiveness, John, and the one person you have to forgive is yourself. You were defending us and you did the right thing. Besides if you hadn't had come looking for me I wouldn't be here today."

John stood up. "Thank you, Mary, I think I've been feeling guilty but now I've got it off my chest I feel better. You are right; the guy was ready to jump when I saw him... I think he had decided."

"Glad to be of help. So do you fancy joining us to discuss holding weddings here? They say hard work never hurt anyone!"

He laughed. "I agree with that, it's also good for the mind."

"Don't forget, John, we are a team, and we all want the best for each other. I'm always here if you need to talk, as are all of us."

"I realise that now and thank you. It means a lot to

know that you all care about me." Mary reached over to hug him and saying,

"It's my pleasure. Come on Alfie, it's your dinner time." she said as they headed for the door. Alfie's ears pricked up at the mention of food, and they both laughed at him.

"I'm coming back as a dog next time," John said. "Life is so much simpler."

*

THE WEDDING

(Il Matrimonio)

The wedding preparations were keeping everyone busy. The paperwork had come through, and the villa was now legally registered to conduct civil wedding ceremonies.

Mary was in Martha's bedroom.

"I know you haven't bought your dress yet, but I wondered if you might be interested in one of my vintage dresses? Of course, my dear, I don't want to put you in a difficult position if you don't like them, but it's just a suggestion."

"Martha, you know me well by now. I would say if I had something else in mind. To be honest, I've been struggling to decide what I want. Can I try some on? I love the vintage look. I'll give Sam and Eva a shout, see if they want to join us."

The cloudy afternoon had turned into a perfect time for a fashion show. Samantha and Eva walked in, Sam carrying a tray of wine glasses and a bottle of Prosecco. They settled themselves in comfy armchairs and watched as Martha set out a variety of dresses on her bed. They were beautiful. Mary touched the delicate materials and, looking at Martha, she said. "I'd love to try this one on."

"Ah, yes, isn't it beautiful. I remember I bought it in

London for the opening of our theatre. It's tight-fitting but, Mary, you are so slim I'm sure it will fit you."

Mary slipped into the dress. It was pure white and clung seductively to her body. The over-dress was hand-stitched lace with an exquisitely patterned detail. The neckline, cut across the shoulder, enhanced Mary's cleavage, and covering the shoulders were delicate drapes of fine lace.

"Well, girls, what's your opinion?" Mary said as she twirled around.

Samantha reached for another glass of Prosecco. She was enjoying this moment.

"It's so you, Mary. You have a classical face and figure. It is perfect."

Eva agreed. "Yes, it looks like it was made for you. You are so beautiful."

"Ah, thank you, guys. Martha, what do you think?" Mary said.

"Darling, Samantha is right. It is a classic look, which suits you. It is quite stunning, but it's not complete. Eva, would you pass me the big box from the cupboard?"

"Gosh, this is so exciting," Eva, said as she helped

273

Martha remove the pink tissue paper to reveal a tight headdress that fitted Mary across her forehead. It was designed in silver filigree and, together with matching earrings, almost completed the outfit.

"One more thing, Mary." Martha unwrapped a pair of elbow-length satin gloves. She added a large bracelet made of the same silver design as the headdress; the 1920s look was complete.

"I love it," Mary shouted in delight. "It's absolutely gorgeous."

*

Christmas Eve and the day of the wedding arrived. The sun was streaming through the bedroom curtains. Mary lay resting, her thoughts focussed on the day ahead.

In her wildest dreams, she didn't believe this day would come. The anticipation of marrying Franco was making her heart race with excitement. She tried not to dwell on the missing years but made a promise to herself that she would from now on make every day special for both of them. A knock at the door made her jump.

"Come in," she said.

Eva entered, carrying a breakfast tray.

"How thoughtful. Come and join me. We've had so little time for a chat lately."

Eva got in the bed with Mary. "I guess you must be feeling very excited. I know I am."

"If anything, I feel nervous, which is not like me. I'll give you a hand with the food. There must be so much to do. I'm so grateful you've given up your Christmas Eve to host our wedding."

"Mary, it is an absolute pleasure for me. I know my dad has only just come into my life, but to see him getting married and to you! Gosh, I can't find the words to say how brilliant it all is. I'm over the moon and I just want this day to be so special for you both. You mustn't worry about anything. It is all under control and there is very little to do. The table is set and looks lovely. It is just last-minute food to organise. Martha has hired extra staff and everyone is busy in the kitchen. She has invited lots of people, so it's going to be a lovely atmosphere. All we need to do is have a relaxing morning and then get dressed. Are you all packed for your honeymoon in Venice?"

"I am. It is going to be so special. I've never been

before. It has always been on my list of places to visit. How about you and your trip to Copenhagen for New Year?"

"Actually, I'm feeling nervous too."

"Oh, you mustn't worry. They will all love you and Henrik will enjoy showing you off to his family."

"That is what is making me feel nervous. His mum is a doctor and his dad is a banker."

"And you, young lady, are a very talented successful chef and a beautiful person. Just look how happy Henrik is. He can't take his eyes off you."

"Really!"

"Yes. There is no need to feel nervous. Just go with it and enjoy being welcomed into a new family."

"I know you are right, but I'm not really into family gatherings. It's all quite new to me." Eva replied.

"I know how you feel. I've never had a family either. But look how we all met a few months ago. We knew nothing about each other, but I consider we are all family now. I think that is important, probably more so than actual blood relatives. Now you have your dad in your life and, I just want you to know how much he loves you and wants the very best for you. He is still overwhelmed you came looking for him and, I know I am biased, but he is a wonderful, kind man and will always be your dad."

Eva moved the tray. "You do realise that from today you will be my step-mum." The two of them lay on the bed, laughing.

"And you, my gorgeous girl, will be my step-daughter! Oh, it's going to be a brilliant day. We both have so much to celebrate and look forward to."

*

Mary stood at the top of the winding staircase. She gasped in amazement at the scene in front of her.

The hall had been decorated with Christmas trees adorned with tiny white fairy lights, simple but very classic. The scent of freshly cut pine trees hung in the air. Large swathes of foliage, with a mixture of sweet-smelling herbs and dried lavender, cascaded down the elegant staircase. It felt like she was in a fairy tale as the sound of a cellist playing softly in the background reached her.

"I can't believe how beautiful the villa looks." She said as she turned to Eva. "You have all worked so hard to create this magic."

"We have enjoyed it, Mary. I'm so glad you like it" Eva surveyed the room. "Oh, look at my papa."

Mary's heart leaped as she saw a very nervous Franco, standing alone underneath the archway of sweet-smelling white roses and foliage, waiting for his bride to join him. His grey suit, white shirt, and a buttonhole of sage eucalyptus and gypsophila complimented his handsome features.

"Come on Mary, my father is waiting for you," Eva

said gently.

Slowly they walked down the staircase, and Franco turned to greet them.

"You take my breath away, Maria. You are so beautiful." He whispered in her ear.

For once, words failed her. Tears of joy appeared in her eyes and she gladly allowed Franco to take the lead, as the realisation this was all real and she was about to be married to the man she had always loved.

The service began, and speaking in Italian, they repeated their vows to each other whilst holding hands. Their guests cheered loudly as Franco kissed his bride and finally they were pronounced husband and wife.

Eva was the first one to hug them both. "I am so happy for you and I wish you years of love and laughter." By this time Franco had tears in his eyes.

Martha stepped forward, her arms stretched out for a hug.

"My beautiful darlings. Many congratulations."

"How can we thank you for this amazing wedding?" Mary said.

"I did very little, just supervised. It was Samantha and

John who did the decorating and, of course, Eva and Henrik prepared the food."

Franco swept the old lady into his arms. "Martha, I love you and you are looking very elegant." He said as he gave her a big kiss.

"Oh, this old thing." Her eyes twinkled with pleasure. "I just found it at the bottom of my suitcase. Although gold has always been a flattering colour for me."

"When she says 'old' she means vintage," Eva interrupted.

"Martha has dressed us all in her treasured clothes and I think we all look amazing, even Alfie who is wearing a bow tie. Look at him, he looks so cute."

"Tutti sembrano fantastici incluso John!" (Everyone looks amazing including John!) Franco replied.

"Did someone mention my name?" John said as he handed out glasses of champagne. "If everyone would like to follow me to the dining area, ladies and gentleman, dinner is served."

John and Henrik had moved a long oak table to the outdoor restaurant underneath the terracing and lemon trees. Elegant decorations adorned the table. To keep the guests warm, a temporary marquee had been constructed and large candles in glass domes were placed around the terrace to give soft and intimate lighting. The weather had been kind to them, as the air was warm in the winter sunshine. The fragrance of citrus fruit hung in the air from the lemon and orange trees, and the sound of music and laughter filled the villa.

Eva had produced an array of traditional Italian and English foods and soon the guests were happily tucking in.

Signor Miccio was having the time of his life. Oh, how he loved a celebration. He was sitting next to Martha, and Mary spotted them having an animated conversation.

"I think Signor Miccio is wooing Martha, Mary laughed as she watched the couple enjoying themselves.

"Of course he is," answered Franco. "He's always had his heart set on her."

Mary smiled. "There is a lot of love in the air. Eva and Henrik only have eyes for each other. And Samantha and Lorenzo, well I think there is a bit of magic happening there as well."

"Oh, I hope so," Franco said.

"I do too. I've been trying my best to get them together for ages. Goodness, all we need to do now is find someone for John."

"John is a man who will decide for himself, although he seems to be enjoying the company of my cousin's daughter, Amelia. I saw them laughing together earlier."

The waiters cleared away the plates, and John arrived pushing a large trolley holding a spectacular wedding cake.

Mary gasped in delight. The cake was three tiers and beautifully decorated.

"I hope you both like it?" Eva said. "I based it on Neapolitan ice cream. The bottom layer is chocolate, the middle strawberry, and the top is vanilla and lemon flavour."

"Darling, it must have taken days to make. It is really stunning. I love the way you have piped the icing to match the lacework on my dress. It is a masterpiece, we can't possibly eat it!"

"You must, but first we need some photographs of the two of you. Here is the knife. Everyone it is cake time."

A hushed silence filled the room as Mary, and Franco

sliced through the layers, which was followed by a tremendous cheer.

"Speech," John cried out.

Franco got to his feet and thanked everyone, but he soon became so overwhelmed with emotion that Mary stood up and took over from him.

"What my husband is trying to say is that he loves you all and we are so delighted you have joined us to celebrate this wonderful day. It means everything to us. I still cannot believe what an incredible year it has been. As you all know, it started when we met Martha, this wonderful woman who invited us into her world and gave us a life-changing opportunity. And, for Eva to be reunited with her father was so special. Now I have married the love of my life, well it has been so amazing. I can't wait to see what happens next year! On a personal level, I discovered what it feels like to be part of a family, and now I have a husband and a daughter. I am the happiest person alive. Thank you, everyone."

Mary sat down and hugged her husband as everyone clapped and cheered.

Signor Miccio stood up and raised a glass to toast the

happy couple. And then the party began in earnest, which continued well into the early hours.

*

Christmas Day dawned and the wedding guests had finally departed in the early hours. Slowly the villa began to wake up. Everyone had slept late, but one by one they were descending on the kitchen for coffee.

"Wasn't it the most beautiful day," Eva said wistfully to Samantha.

"And didn't we do it well? I'm amazed at the talent we all have for organising such an event. I can't wait to start doing weddings. Are you going to put some photographs on the website? It will look stunning."

"Yes, I'll do that. Next year is going to be such fun" Eva replied as she prepared a breakfast tray for Martha." Do you want anything to eat, Sam?"

"Thanks, but I don't think I could face anything at the moment. Look at the state of the place. It's going to take us ages to sort this out."

"I think we should leave all the flowers up. They look so lovely. It won't take us long to get organised, then, we'll have to get dinner on the go. Shall we aim for 4pm?"

At that moment, Alfie ran through the door with John close behind.

"Merry Christmas everyone," John said. "How are you all? No hangovers?"

"Merry Christmas John. Come and have some coffee." Sam said as she passed him the coffee pot. "We were just talking about getting the place sorted so we can all sit down for dinner later."

"That sounds great, I'm hungry already! "

"What, after that huge feast we had yesterday. You can't be!" Eva laughed.

"Alfie and I have been up for hours. We've had a long walk down to the sea, haven't we old chap." John patted Alfie on the head and in return the little dog stared up at him with affection.

Mary and Franco came into the room hand in hand.

"Merry Christmas, guys," Mary's smile was infectious. "How are you all?"

"I think we are still in wedding mode. We can't get over how brilliant it was." Sam said as she headed out of the door with a breakfast tray in her hand. "I'm just going to see how Martha is this morning."

"Oh, tell her we'll be up to see her in a little while. We want to thank her again for making our day so perfect."

"So when does the honeymoon start?" John filled two more cups with coffee and handed them over.

"Our flight is tomorrow, at 1 pm," Franco said. "We thought we would help clear everything up and if it's ok, join you all for Christmas dinner. Then we'll spend the night at the house in Marina Grande so we can set off straight from there."

"Oh, that sounds really exciting." Eva gave her father a hug. "You'll have a wonderful time. Don't forget to send us photos on your phone. We will want to know what you are both up to."

"We certainly will, especially the one of Franco serenading me on a gondola." Mary laughed. "I'm getting used to being on boats."

"And in return, I'll send you one of Henrik and me in Copenhagen. We set off tomorrow as well."

"Cara mio. You will love it. Denmark is a beautiful country and Henrik has assured me he will take excellent care of you."

   "Oh papa, of course he will."

*

The day passed by at a leisurely rate. Everyone helped to bring the villa back to normality whilst Eva prepared the Christmas lunch. Their laughter filled the air and after the presents were distributed from underneath the sweet smelling Christmas tree, they settled in front of the fire until it was time for Franco and Mary to leave.

As they drove away, Mary whispered to Franco.

"Do you mind if we make a small stop at the Monastery? There is something I want to do."

"Of course, it's on our way."

"Thanks. I telephoned the Abbott earlier and asked if it was all right to visit Giovanni's grave. I spoke to John recently about him and something has been on my mind so I just want to put things right."

A short while later Franco stopped outside the imposing building. "Do you want me to come with you?"

"Yes please, it won't take a moment."

They reached the simple grave and Mary laid a spray of wild flowers on the mound. She reached in her pocket and pulled out the silver necklace and placed it over the wooden cross.

"The police sent it back to me and, to be honest, I

didn't know what to do with it. I certainly could never wear it again, so I thought it should go back to Giovanni. For some reason, I feel sorry for him and it just seems to be the right thing to do."

Franco stared at her. "Well, I can't say I understand, but if it helps you to find peace then it is the right thing to do."

"Strangely, this young man has brought us together and yes, I do feel it puts a final ending to such a sad life."

They stood holding hands and both silently said a prayer of forgiveness.

*

NEW YEAR'S
EVE
(Vigilia di Capodanno)

Sundays had become a time to down tools and relax, especially after a long lunch. A fire was blazing in the sitting room, and Martha and Samantha were relaxing on the over sized settees.

"Hi," John said as he came in to join them. He had been working in his workshop. One of the fashionable boutique shops in Sorrento had placed an order for ten handbags, and John had almost finished. It gave him space to enjoy something important to him, and he was glad he could indulge in his hobby and make some extra money.

"Come and sit down. Move over, Alfie, let John see the fire." Alfie was reluctant to leave his nice, comfortable spot until Martha picked him up and he settled on her lap.

"Would you like a crumpet, John? I'm toasting them by the fire. It gives them an unusual smoky flavour." Sam laughed. "I'm sure Eva would be impressed. The tea is still hot if you want a cup."

"Yes, please." John poured himself a drink.

"We were just wondering how Eva is enjoying Copenhagen? I am so glad she has met Henrik. He is such a nice young man." Martha said. "She deserves someone special in her life."

"Don't forget her dad, Martha," Sam replied. "I still can't get over the coincidence of her meeting him and then Mary coming back into his life. It is so romantic."

"And wasn't it the most beautiful wedding?" John interrupted. "I hope we get some bookings to hold weddings here in the villa. It would add something special and I think we did it very well."

"I'm sure we will," Martha replied. "It's a great idea, and the villa is the perfect setting. Changing the subject, how did your meeting go with the Viticulturist, John?"

"What is one of those?" Sam inquired as she passed over a plate of hot, burnt crumpets to John.

"He advises on the production of grapes. He thinks the vineyard is not too bad and the grape quality could be good enough to produce a decent wine."

"That's good news. My father used to produce excellent wine. There was an annual grape treading festival. In those days, it was the highlight of the harvest time. Villagers would come from miles around to help pick the grapes and watch as the 'tramplers' - the experts

- did their 'dance'. It was exciting and an occasion where all the locals helped each other. There was a lot of sampling going off, too. Even the young children drank a small glass, although watered down, of course. My father gave most of his wine away, saving a few bottles for the family. I think there may be a bottle or two still in the cellar."

"What wonderful memories, Martha. Do you find Sorrento has changed a lot over the years?" Sam asked.

"Yes, it has, but with the tourist industry, it has brought prosperity to the area, and that has to be a good thing. You can still find the traditional way of life in the villages up in the mountains. The terracing lends itself to the old ways and, of course, fruit picking is still a seasonal event."

"We should tell Eva and Henrik. They could mention it in their blog."

"That's a good idea. How is it going?" John said as he spread a heap of butter on his crumpet.

"It's attracting a lot of attention online, especially the website. Lots of inquiries from people who want to come and stay or visit the restaurant. Henrik's friend has done a superb job setting it up for them. Have you seen it yet Martha?"

"Yes, dear. Eva showed me. I loved the bright colours, and the villa looks spectacular. Isn't it funny how we've just been talking about the old ways and compared to modern life, there is such a difference. I'm so glad I've lived to experience both."

"It is the way forward. Eva was showing me her ideas for a cookery book. I'm hoping one day we can do one about wine making, although I've still got a lot to learn." John said.

"Well, you must get Franco to take you up to the rural villages and help with the grape festival. You would love it and Henrik too."

"Thanks, Martha, that's a great idea."

"How are you enjoying working in the hospital, Samantha, dear?"

"I love it, although three days a week is enough. All the staff are wonderful and so friendly. It's easy work. They send all the complicated cases to Naples. I was telling Lorenzo about it the other day. He thinks I should be in Naples with him. It is a much bigger hospital, but at the moment, I'm happy with the delivery of babies and all the minor problems that happen. People still need nursing."

"Any news from Mary and Franco?"

"Yes, Martha. I got a text message to say they were having a wonderful time. The hotel is on the Grand Canal. She is going to ring us later to wish us a Happy New Year."

"Oh, that's wonderful. Venice is the perfect place for a honeymoon. It is so unique."

"How are you celebrating New Year's Eve tonight?" John said as he helped himself to a piece of Christmas cake.

"We've just been saying it's going to be quiet without Eva and Mary. If the rain keeps off, we might go on the roof terrace and enjoy the fireworks. Do you want to join us John?"

"I'd love to. I've never been fond of New Year's Eve, but this has been such a fantastic year and with all our plans for the future, I think it would be nice to toast in 2020."

"Yes, John, it would be a shame to miss it."

The heat from the fire was being to relax them.

"This is lovely music, Sam," Martha said as she curled her feet up on the sofa.

"It's the BBC overseas service. They are playing popular songs from the decades."

Martha closed her eyes to the strains of Matt Monroe singing 'On Days Like These.' John and Samantha did the same as the warmth from the fire and the descending dusk made it difficult to stay awake.

The six o'clock news came on the radio.

"This is the BBC in London
Here are your headlines"

"People around the world are ringing in the New Year as 2019 ends. Magnificent firework displays attracted enormous crowds in Australia and New Zealand. London is expecting a high number of people this evening to welcome in the new decade.

Other news. The Chinese Authorities have alerted the World Health Organisation of a potential unidentified virus that has caused an unprecedented outbreak of pneumonia cases in Wuhan City, China. There are no further details at the moment, but we are expecting an update tomorrow."

THE END
(LA FINE)

Acknowledgements

My first introduction to Sorrento was in 1969. At 18, my friend, Christine, and I left our office jobs in England, and bought one-way train tickets to Sorrento to head off for an adventure. We had applied for work, in a hotel in Sant'Agnello. On arrival, we were told our jobs had gone to someone else. We had no money, no mobile phones (not in those days), but we survived and spent four happy summer seasons working together in hotels. Fifty years later, we are still close friends and, as the song says, we 'Ritorno a Sorrento' whenever we can.

To my daughter Carrie, and my husband, Barrie. Thank you for your constant support, encouragement and inspiration in all my writing and artistic endeavours.

Finally, my wonderful mum, Joan, who inspired our family with her passion for art and love of Italy, and opera. Her spirit is now flying high over the Amalfi coast, where we carried out her wishes and scattered her ashes.

1969 – Chris and I in our silver service waitress
uniforms

Printed in Great Britain
by Amazon